the last daughter

RENÉE WALKER

www.reneewalkerwriterpoet.com

Books by Renée Walker:
Texas Rangeland
Hill Country & Other Poems
Around the Square: That's Mason

Printing and e-book distribution by
CreateSpace, Charleston, South Carolina.

Book design, photography and production
by Julie Mader-Meersman, Originalia.

CONTENTS

EMILY | *Chapters 1–5* | 2

MARY H | *Chapter 6* | 38

RHODA | *Chapters 7–9* | 50

ANN | *Chapters 10–14* | 76

KITTY | *Chapters 15–17* | 114

STEED | *Chapters 18–25* | 136

Epilogue | 201

Night is drawing nigh.
How long the road is.
But, for all the time the journey
has already taken,
How you have needed every second of it.

— **DAG HAMMARSKJÖLD**

FAMILY TREE

EMILY LOWERY + JOHN BOY RAY

14 children } *Matilda C, Patterson McNeal,*
Leonard Lafayette, **Mary Hazelton,**
Gincy Abegill, Miranda Brown,
Jelanor Victoria, Losen Van Buren,
Marshall, Narsis, Willard, Eudora,
Vines, John Pinkard

MARY H RAY + NEWTON MARSHAL STEED

10 children } *Lafayette (Fate), R.L. (Vert),*
Missouri Lee, **Rhoda Florence,**
Ada V, C. Fernando, Noland McNeel,
Hilman, Clevy, Pearly B

RHODA STEED + WILLIAM JAMES SISTRUNK

9 children } *Willie Blanton, Ruby May,*
Mary T, Jimmie Nita, Ole Detmer,
Annie Beatrice, *Everly James,*
Jonnie True, Frances Lawana

ANN SISTRUNK + WILLIAM W. CLOCK

2 Children } *William, Jr.,* **Kitty Annabelle**

KITTY CLOCK + JAMES BRUCE GAULDEN

2 Children } *Will,* **Steed**

STEED GAULDEN

} *The Last Daughter*

Emily

1

Twenty-three girls in the town of Fayette were named Emily. I was one
of them.

Mama gave birth to both of us before the first frost. "Twins are a curse,"
Granny always contended. "Especially if they're girls."

Pa said, "At least they arrived early."

That winter of 1824 turned colder than expected.

"You listen to me, Joseph Lowrey. Those girls will do nothing but bring bad
luck. That's why we had such a hard winter. It's their doing. If they
had come on time, we'd all been spared the suffering." It was a
common comment.

"Yes, Mother Daughtry," Pa would reply, then look at Mama and wink. But
Mama never smiled back.

"Stand still, Emily," Granny scolded.

"It hurts."

"Stop sniveling."

She brushed my hair so hard I thought it would pull right out of my head.
I fought the tears.

"Hush or I'll give you something to cry about."

Granny parted my straight black hair down the middle with a sharp comb
as I screamed. Every morning we went through this painful ritual,
she pulling, me screaming.

"Stop that!" she'd snap, whacking my head with the back of the brush.

I'd stare at Mama who stood at the stove, her back to me, tending to the fire, stirring the bubbling cast iron pot while bouncing the youngest boy on her hip.

She'd whip the hair into a straight braid that hung heavy against my back like a big old rope. It was pulled back so tight it caused my eyes to pop open so wide I couldn't even blink.

"A red ribbon on the end would look so pretty!" I said one morning

Mama cast an eye at me as if I'd asked for a silver coin or my own pony. Pa finished eating and rose from the table.

"Emily Ann Lowrey," Granny growled. "Shame on you. Look at your pa leaving early every day just so he can put food on this table for you to eat. He does not break his back working to put ribbons on a little girl's hair. Now stop this nonsense. Mark my words, Lucinda. Girls are nothing but trouble."

"Yes, Mother," Mama sighed, switching the baby to her other hip.

Pa winked at me as he put on his hat.

I squirmed away from Granny but she managed to smack me on the rear with her brush as the door closed behind Pa.

———————

My twin sister died the year of the bad drought.

By then, Mama had six more babies. All of them boys.

"Mark my words, Joseph Lowrey. Those twins have been a curse since day one," Granny exclaimed as she shoved me into a black dress that tied up the back with a smooth black cord. "That sickly girl nearly wore us all out."

I stood still as a post while Granny spit on her hands and slicked my hair down. She eyed me as I stared straight ahead, not moving, not crying, not caring what she did.

Go ahead. Hit me, I thought to myself. I will never cry again.

Death, frequent caller in Fayette, did not spare a single family and no one could turn away from the knock on the door. Pa used to say Death took no prisoners. And then Death came one day and it took my sister. I never could understand why He didn't take old Granny. No. Death wanted my sister instead. She was young, quiet, and kind. Matilda never complained, although she never did breathe easy the entire time she was alive.

Mama constantly rubbed stuff on her chest that made everybody's eyes water but the coughing and choking persisted. Granny would watch Mama and just shake her head and walk away. Mama tried hot mustard plasters and hot water bottles. Vinegar baths and wet tea leaves. Raising her head up. Laying her flat. Thumping her on the back. Patting her on the chest. She even tried packing snow on her one year. Poor Matilda. Nothing helped. No doctor could fix her.

Every once in a great while if the weather was fine and I had all the housework and washing and ironing caught up, Mattie and I would go down through the woods to the creek. She loved it there. So did I, but it was especially good for her to be there by the flowing water and nothing but the leaves stirring in the nice warm breeze all around us. The two of us would sit there and watch a twig or leaf float by on the water. We might even see some fish or hear a hawk or watch a redbird hop among the fallen limbs.

Matilda always breathed easy there beside the creek. I used to imagine how nice it would be if she could stay down there. I pictured a cabin with a long pulley that went all the way up to the house and I could send food down to her in a dinner pail. But pretty soon the serenity would be broken by Granny's voice, yelling for us to get back to the house and our chores.

By the time we walked back up to the house, Matilda had to be helped into bed and comforted with hot honey water. Then I would get pulled outside and given a whipping. But I never did mind. Just so long as Matilda was all right.

"Maybe we'll get some rain now that one of you is gone," Granny hissed in my ear as she pushed me away. "There now, Lucinda," the old woman said loudly to my mother, "this one's ready for the funeral. I'll just get my hat."

"Mama, may I walk with you and Pa?" I pictured myself between them, left hand in Pa's and my right one in Mama's as though it was just the three of us.

"No, Emily," she sighed. "You take care of the older boys and keep behind us. And keep them out of trouble or Granny will get after you."

Pa held the door while Mama picked up the baby and straddled him on her hip, her black cape swaddling it. Granny took the hand of the toddler and they all filed out the door. Me and the four boys followed.

———

That summer it rained. And rained. It rained till all the old people said the drought was finally over. That was the summer I met John Boy Ray. He came to Pa's blacksmith shop. I'd say he stood near as tall as Pa even though he wasn't much older than me. What I noticed first was his hands. They had seen work but still had a kind of beauty to them. Different than Pa's somehow. His long fingers fascinated me. So did his strong nose and deep-set eyes.

"Here's your dinner, Pa. Mama says to eat it while it's hot."

Pa did not look up nor cease forging the blazing hot iron.

I set the tin pail on the nearby workbench and patted the top to make sure the lid was on tight. Then I noticed the stranger standing in one corner of the shop staring at me.

I looked left and right and back at the young man and then at my father and then down at my dress.

"Oh no!" I cried. Mud was splattered down the front of my muslin apron.

"What's wrong?" Pa didn't like being interrupted from his work.

"Nothing, Pa! Nothing." I tried to brush the apron clean, but only managed to smear the dirt.

When I glanced up, the stranger was smiling back at me. I didn't know whether to smile or run out of the barn.

With tongs he had forged himself, Pa pulled the metal bit off the hot anvil and set it aside to cool.

"Now then, what's all the fuss?" Pa asked again.

"Nothing, sir," I replied, returning my gaze downward.

"Young man," he turned to the stranger, "if you could come back before
    dark I should have everything else fixed up for you."

"Yessir."

"What did you say your name was again?"

"John Boy, sir. John Boy Ray."

"Mighty fine. This here's my daughter, Emily Ann Lowrey."

"Miss Lowrey," the young man said, bowing his head.

I nearly fell over at the sound of his voice.

"Emily, don't be rude. Say hello to the gentleman."

"Hello, sir," I managed to mumble.

"The young man laughed. "Call me John Boy."

Pa came over and took the lunch pail from me. "How old are you, boy?"

"Nineteen, sir."

"Mighty fine, mighty fine. Well, if you will excuse me I am going to eat my
    dinner so I can get back to work so that you can be on your way."

"Yessir."

"You can get something to eat down the road."

"That sounds fine, sir."

"Emily," Pa turned to me. "You take John Boy here and show him where
    Mrs. Barfield's place is."

"But Pa…"

"Don't worry about your mother. I'll explain why you were late getting
    back. Now get going."

I stood transfixed, staring at John Boy.

"Take that boy before he faints from hunger. And then get on home."

"Yes, Pa."

Before he could change his mind, I dashed out the door. Poor John Boy
    had to hurry to catch up with me

"Miss Lowrey, could we please slow down?"

"Sorry, sir." I slackened my pace, but only slightly.

"Please, call me John Boy."

"Yes sir." I still couldn't look at him, but I could feel his gaze on me.

"If I may be so bold, how old are you?"

"Seventeen, sir. I mean…John Boy." I felt the redness rise to my cheeks.

"Have you lived in Fayette all your life?"

"I have."

"I'm from the East," John Boy volunteered. "From North Carolina."

"I see," I replied.

"But I'm headed out West."

"West! What is west of here?" I wondered. "So many people talk about going west. Everybody wants to go out west. And so many, like yourself, pass through Fayette. Why is it nobody seems to go east? Why west?"

John Boy suddenly stopped walking. "You mean you don't know?"

I kept on walking. I knew I'd pay a price for getting home late.

"No, I don't know!" I called back.

He ran to catch up with me.

"Why, it's open territory. A man can make a life for himself. Any kind of life he wants. I've worked as a striker before so I can even open my own blacksmith shop if I want. Where I'm headed they say it's full of so much timber you can never cut it all down."

"And where might that be?" I stopped walking. We had arrived in front of Barfield's Dining Room.

"They call it Mississippi. Just over them mountains there," John Boy said, gesturing at the peaks that rose above the town.

I stared at the endless sky above the mountains that went higher than high, from blue to black. It seemed impossible to grasp.

The courthouse tower bonged out one o'clock.

"I must go!" I screamed and took off down the road and never looked back.

John Boy stood there until Emily disappeared around the corner. She's a little thing, he thought, and female at that. But she runs faster than any man I've ever seen.

Then he went inside to eat.

2

"Mama! Mama, I'm home!" I yelled, slamming the door behind me.

No one answered.

"Mama?"

I looked in the bedrooms. The two youngest were asleep, oblivious to the world. I went on out the back door to the washhouse.

"Mama?"

From out of the dark corner, Granny hurled herself at me.

"Look at you! Where have you been?" the old woman screamed. "Leaving me to do all the wash. The Lord shall punish thee! You are nothing but evil! Ever since the day you were born!"

"Granny, no!" I ducked as the old woman swung at me.

"You are late! Late late late! What have you been doing? You can't fool me!"

I dodged her and rushed for the door.

"Oh no you don't, you little tart. You dirty, nasty girl. Granny's going to teach you once and for all, you bad, evil girl!"

I tripped on the wooden bench and fell face down on the stone floor. The old woman grabbed my hair and twisted it into a hard, tight bun.

"I've had enough of you! There will be no more disobedience, do you hear me?" she screamed.

"Granny, I'm sorry! Please let me go! Please don't hurt me! I didn't do anything!"

My mother was not there to save me this time. She had packed a lunch and
taken the four older boys down to the creek for a couple of hours to
swim, fish, and check their traps for rabbits and squirrels.

If only they returned now, they would hear me screaming.

Granny dragged me across the washroom floor and banged my head against
the iron sink. I fought and kicked and nearly got loose but the old woman
still had hold of my hair.

"You must pay for your sins!"

"I didn't do anything, Granny! Please don't! No!"

The old woman, amazingly strong and nimble for her age, kicked and kicked
until I no longer screamed or cried.

"There, you little tramp. You ungrateful, dirty girl," she said, spitting on me.
"That will learn you. There will be no more filth in this house!"

Granny straightened the ruffled cap over her wiry gray hair and smoothed
the apron strapped across her round, distended belly. Calmly, quietly, she
walked out of the washhouse and paused to glance west towards the
creek just as Mama appeared on the edge of the woods. The boys came
running up behind her, chasing each other, laughing, with fish swinging
from their poles.

"Granny! Granny!" they cried. "Look what all we caught!"

The old woman smiled and clapped her hands with excitement. "Emily!" she yelled
back towards the wash house. "Better get going! You got fish to clean!"

The boys clambered up the back steps and into the house with Granny
following behind, clucking at them all the way.

Mama hesitated on the back step. She sensed something was terribly wrong. I
slowly emerged from the washhouse, holding my sides in pain. My black hair
now untwisted, rose from my head, tangled in every direction. One eye had
already swelled half-closed, a purple-black encircling it. I looked up to see
my mother biting her lip, holding onto the railing with all blood drained from
her face, her eyes numb and gray.

"Mama," I pleaded, faintly.

Just then the youngest child waddled to the door crying for her. Mama wearily
turned and went inside.

I didn't know my life would change that day. The forever and ever kind
of change. I thought my fate was set like those heavy locks that
Pa forges for people who have special things to put up. It's curious
how folks get all that fancy stuff, china dishes, special firearms, fine
paintings big as a door, silk dresses, strings of gold and pearls, and
then pay Pa good money to make it so they can lock it all up.

Being the oldest, and the only girl, I was taught since childhood to help
with all the chores and all the children. It was my duty, and my fate
as a female. May God forgive me for saying this, but sometimes I
think Matilda was lucky to have passed on so soon.

I long to be able to read a book but there is never any time. Besides, the
only book in the house is the Bible. And it belongs to Granny. She
never lets anyone touch it. Not even Pa. It was the only thing she
had left from her journey to America. She tells the story over and
over to anybody who will stop long enough for her to grab hold of
them. And believe me, she has told it a time or two.

I miss Matilda more than anyone can ever know. We knew each other's
thoughts and feelings without ever having to speak. Once we fell
to giggling for no real reason and just couldn't stop. If Pa hadn't
walked in right then, Granny would've given us a good beating. Or
me, at least. Matilda never did breathe real well so Granny pretty
much let her be and gave me her share instead.

I couldn't wait until dark each day after the boys were finally put to bed and
I got all the supper pots and plates washed and put up, then I could
finally join my sister. Granny slept in the nursery with the two youngest.
The other four boys took up one bedroom. Mama and Pa had the main
bedroom. Mattie and I slept together in the sunroom off the parlor.

I loved and hated that room. Most of the year the morning light burst
over us, warming our bed and filling the room with such a splendid
brightness that I felt sure it would cure Matilda. I would take
deep breaths trying to suck the warm light down into my heart. I
encouraged Mattie to do the same but she would fall to coughing.
But all those windows made the room bitterly cold in the winter. We

hung heavy quilts to block the freezing dampness, which also blocked any sunlight. It didn't really matter where Matilda slept. The doctor told Mama what Matilda had would never go away. So the sickness took Matilda away instead. Forever. And little did I know that in a few hours something would take me away forever, too.

I cleaned all the fish, dredged them in cornmeal, and fried them up. I boiled potatoes, taking a few out ahead of time so I could slice and fry them in bacon fat. I mashed and whipped the rest of the potatoes for the children. I lifted the fried potatoes out onto a plate, added water and flour to the pan, and stirred up gravy for the boys.

"I guess your Pa has somebody waiting on him," Mama sighed. She sat in the rocker with the youngest asleep in her lap. "It's going to be dark soon. He should have been along already."

"Don't go to fretting now," Mother Daughtry admonished her daughter. "Emily!" The old woman quickly turned her focus on me.

"Yes ma'am," I murmured.

"I'll see to it the boys finish their supper. You go see about your Pa."

"Yes ma'am." I tried to restrain myself. Any reason to get away from the house was a blessing.

"Slow down, Miss Priss," the old woman commanded.

Mama just kept rocking and staring out the window.

"Take a dinner pail and fill it up for your Pa just in case he's got to keep on working. You know he works night and day for you, young lady, just so you can have food and clothing and a roof over your head."

"Yes, ma'am," I muttered.

"And don't you ever forget it."

"Yes, ma'am," I sighed.

"Well, don't just stand there ma'am-ing me. Get going!"

I tried my best not to rattle the pans as I hurriedly filled the dinner pail.

"I don't see you gone!" the old woman hollered.

"I'm going!" I cried. I flew out the door, the dinner pail swinging in my hand.

Before I left I heard Granny say, "That girl is more trouble than she's
worth." Then, "You look kind of peaked, Lucinda. Is it your time?"

Mama kept rocking and shook her head and tears began to stream
down her face. "I'm with child, Mother," she said without feeling. I
stopped and looked through the window.

Granny clapped her hands. "The Lord has blessed us once again!"

Mama just kept shaking her head.

"Boys!" the old woman cried. "Your Mama's going to have a new baby!
Let's hope it's a boy! And you all will have another brother."

My brothers nodded with disinterest and went on eating.

"It might be nice to have a little girl," Mama said softly. "To take Matilda's
place."

"Don't be ridiculous, Lucinda. Girls are nothing but trouble. We must pray
hard for a boy. And we must pray extra hard it isn't twins."

Mama's tears kept flowing.

"Now don't worry about a thing. Emily's a strong girl. Stubborn and ill
behaved, mind you. But she can handle all the children without my
help. That frees me to care for the newborn. We'll be fine. You'll see."

Mama went on rocking and weeping.

I took off running.

3

All the way to the blacksmith shop I imagined my father dead or badly
      burned and all alone, in pain, dying.

"Pa! Pa!" I bolted through the door nearly knocking down John Boy Ray.

My father was bent over near the blazing coals, hammering.

"Pa, you're alright!" I gasped with relief.

He kept his eyes on his work. "Yes, daughter. I'm fine."

"Mama was worried."

"I knew she would be. But I can't leave this man stranded, now can I?"

 "No, sir," I said, glancing at John Boy.

"Good evening, Miss Lowrey," he said.

My eyes darted from him to Papa and back.

"Good evening, sir," I curtsied.

"You forgot already? Call me John Boy," he smiled.

"John Boy," I said softly. My face burned even though I stood away from the fire.

Papa laid his hammer down. "I think that ought to do you, young fella."

"I brought you supper, Pa." I suddenly remembered the pail I was holding. "The
      boys caught some fish today."

I set the pail on the workbench under the bright kerosene light. Papa and
      John Boy saw my blackened eye, swollen cheek, and how I grabbed
      my torso.

John Boy watched from the dark corner of the shop as Papa examined my

face under the light. I cried out when he felt my ribs. Papa slowly
lowered himself onto the nearby bench.

"Something's got to be done," he mumbled to himself, holding his head in
his rough, blackened hands.

"It's alright, Pa."

"No," he shook his head. "No, Emily. It is not alright." His voice grew tense.
"It has never been alright."

He took me by the arm and gently pulled me in front of him.

"Mr. Ray, would you please come over here?"

The young man did as requested.

"Stand here, please. Beside my daughter."

We stood together, side by side, as if at an altar.

I had never seen my father so serious or concerned.

Papa took a deep breath and we waited for him to speak.

"John Boy Ray," he said. "You strike me as a good man. A man with both
faith and good sense. From what you have told me, I believe you are
intent on making a life for yourself where you are headed. You are
young and strong. Emily here is also young and strong."

He stared hard at me, his wounded daughter. "Yes, she is very strong.
And she will make you a good wife."

John Boy coughed with surprise.

"Pa!" I cried.

"Now hear me out, Daughter. This is your chance. I wondered how it
would appear. And when. But I have prayed for it and knew in my
heart one day your time would finally arrive."

Papa looked directly at John Boy, "Mr. Ray, do you understand what I am
saying here?"

John Boy turned and looked at my beaten face and then looked back at
her father.

"Yes sir, I understand."

"Emily, I want you to go with him. God willing, you will have a good life.
You won't if you stay here."

"But Pa," I protested, throwing myself on him.

"Be strong, Daughter. Make your old Pa proud."

"What about Mama? She needs my help."

"Don't you worry about that."

"But I need to tell her goodbye."

"No, I will tell her for you." Papa carefully raised me back on to my feet beside John Boy.

John Boy gently took my hand.

"Mr. Ray, I want you to marry her as soon as you get over those mountains."

"You have my word, sir."

"And you will not touch my daughter until the both of you are legally man and wife in the eyes of God. Do I have your promise on that?"

I stared at the dirt floor.

John Boy nodded. "Yes sir, as God is my witness. I will take care of your daughter."

"Good. You better get your horse, son."

As soon as John Boy left the shop, Papa embraced me as I silently wept.

"Your mama will be wondering what's keeping both of us."

We didn't know Mama had already sent the oldest boy to fetch us.

Papa opened a metal box on the workbench and lifted out a small pistol. He checked to be sure it was loaded and then thrust it at me.

"Keep this on you," he said.

Shocked, I immediately stuck it in my apron.

"And do not be afraid to use it."

"Yes, Pa."

"On anyone who tries to hurt you. Do you take my meaning?"

"Yes, Pa."

Then my father reached into the same box and took out a tiny Bible. He paused over it a moment before handing it to me.

"This was my mother's. I wish you could have known her. You remind me of her in so many ways. She would have adored you."

I held the Bible close to my aching torso. I noticed a red ribbon dangling from inside the closed book and opened it to where the ribbon lay.

"Psalm 91," Papa said. "It was your grandmother's favorite. May it guide you all the rest of your days, my child. And keep you safe and sound."

"Oh, Pa. Thank you."

John Boy Ray trotted into the shop on his horse. Papa helped me mount up behind the young man. He handed John Boy a small leather pouch full of coins.

"This should help you get to where you are going."

I shoved the Bible deep inside my apron next to the pistol.

"Here, Daughter. You take the supper."

I grabbed hold of the tin pail, tears running down my face.

"You better get!'

"Pa! Pa!" We heard the oldest boy cry out as he neared the shop.

"Go! Now!" Papa slapped the back of the horse and John Boy Ray and I took off into the darkness. "May Godspeed!" I heard from the darkness.

Then Pa did something amazing; he picked up his rifle and started to go after us just as my brother ran into the blacksmith shop. Pa shot three times, pointing it just slightly left so the bullets would lodge in the hay bales.

4

We rode for days.

Nights we spent sleeping out under the stars.

I cried the first night.

I never had spent one single night away from my folks. Never.

Now I was riding horseback with a stranger, a man, and we were riding away, further and further away, from my home.

I had to put my arms around him to hold on. And I didn't even know him.

The first night we stopped high up in the mountains. It was just too dark and too cold to keep on.

John Boy Ray laid out his bedroll on the ground for me to sleep on. He never touched me and I tried not to look at him. He bundled himself up in his coat as best he could and slept propped up against a big pine tree.

I was so worn out but my head was spinning. I finally cried myself to sleep.

We traveled on this way. Not talking. Just climbing up and up the trail.

Sometimes when it got slow going, I got off the horse and walked for a ways.

The mountains are beautiful.

They hold all the trees.

And the trees are so tall they seem to hold up the sky.

We wound our way through the pines.

"You seem to know where you are going," I called.

John Boy and the horse had gotten up to the top of the ridge ahead of me.

"I thought you said you'd never been to Mississippi," I added.

"I haven't. But I figure we have to go up in order to go down!"

I sat down to catch my breath.

John Boy dismounted.

"C'mon, horse," he said, and tied the reins to a tree branch.

"You mean we won't be living up here in the mountains?" I asked.

"No, Miss Emily. Where we're headed is down on the other side."

"That's disappointing," I sighed.

John Boy sat down beside me.

"Look around us," he said. "Do you see a town?

I shook my head.

"Do you see a church?"

"No."

"Or a way stop?"

I shook my head and fought back the tears.

"I don't mean to upset you, Miss. But it's pretty clear we can't stay here."

"But it's so majestic," I said. "Look around us. Look at all the beautiful tall,
green trees. And look up at that sky. You can almost touch it, it's so
close. It takes my breath away."

"That's because we're on top of the mountain," he said. "The air is thinner
way up high."

I looked right at him. "Has nothing ever taken your breath away, sir? And
I don't mean being on top of a mountain, either."

John Boy sat there and thought long and hard but made no reply.

"Hasn't there ever been one single moment or incident in your life...or
maybe a sound like music or the running of a creek...or the sight of
something that made you gasp, it was so wonderful, so powerful?"

He shook his head. "No, Miss Emily. Can't say as there has been."

I felt sorry for him right then. But I said no more.

I reached into my apron. "My daddy gave me this Bible just before we left."

"That looks like a fine one," John Boy said.

"It was his mother's. The grandmother I never knew."

I tried not to cry.

"I miss Pa."

John Boy just stared at me.

"I miss my mother too," I said.

He picked up a long twig and started breaking it into little pieces.

"What about your folks?" I asked.

John Boy just kept snapping off bits of twig and tossing them out in front of him.

"Are they still living?"

John Boy shrugged. "Don't rightly know," he said.

"Where did they live?"

"Back the way I came from."

"In Carolina?"

"Yes, ma'am."

He kept on breaking bits of twig.

"Sir, are you running from something?"

John Boy flung the rest of the twig as far as he could.

"Why do you ask me a thing like that?" he demanded.

"Because my daddy trusted me to you. And he is a good man. And you gave him your word you would take care of me and not harm me."

John Boy jumped up. "And have I not done that?"

"Please, sir. Do not use that tone of voice with me."

"I told you to stop calling me 'sir.'"

"I am not afraid of you, John Boy Ray. My granny taught me all about fear."

I had not thought of her since we left Fayette and now I suddenly felt sick to my stomach. I could spit on her. It was because of her that Pa sent me away.

John Boy wandered over to the horse.

I opened the little Bible to Psalm 91 as Pa had told me to do and began reading it aloud:

He that dwelleth in the secret place of the most High shall abide under the shadow of the Almighty.

I will say of the Lord, He is my refuge and my fortress:

My God; in him will I trust.

Surely he shall deliver thee from the snare of the fowler, and from the noisome pestilence.

He shall cover thee with his feathers, and under his wings shalt
thou trust: his truth shall be thy shield and buckler.

I glanced at John Boy. He sat on the ground rubbing the horse's muzzle.
I continued reading even louder than before:

Thou shalt not be afraid for the terror by night; nor for the arrow
that flieth by day;
Nor for the pestilence that walketh in darkness; nor for the
destruction that wasteth at noonday.

John Boy chimed in, reciting each word along with me as I read on:

A thousand shall fall at thy side, and ten thousand at thy right
hand; but it shall not come nigh thee.
Only with thine eyes shalt thou behold and see the reward of
the wicked.
Because thou hast made the Lord, which is my refuge, even
the most High, thy habitation;
There shall no evil befall thee, neither shall any plague come
nigh thy dwelling.

I stopped and looked at him but he did not look my way.
I continued but he remained silent:

For he shall give his angels charge over thee, to keep thee in all
thy ways.
They shall bear thee up in their hands, lest thou dash thy foot
against a stone.

"I like that part," I said. "I believe in angels. Don't you?"
John Boy said nothing.
I read the lines again:

For he shall give his angels charge over thee, to keep thee in
all thy ways.
They shall bear thee up in their hands, lest thou dash thy foot

against a stone.

Thou shalt tread upon the lion and adder: the young lion and the
dragon shalt thou trample under feet.

Because he hath set his love upon me, therefore will I deliver him:
I will set him on high, because he hath known my name.

He shall call upon me, and I will answer him: I will be with him in
trouble; I will deliver him, and honor him.

With long life will I satisfy him, and show him my salvation.

I closed the book.

"Amen," I said.

"Amen," John Boy said softly.

He stood up and untied the horse.

"We better get," he said as he flung his leg over the saddle.

"Yessir," I replied and got to my feet.

I tucked the little Bible safely back in my apron. John Boy extended his hand.
I grabbed hold with both of mine and he pulled me up behind him.

"I know a man who settled in Mississippi," John Boy called over his shoulder.

Slowly we were making our way down the other side of the mountain.

"I'm hoping he will give me work or help me find some."

I tried not to hold on to John Boy too tightly whenever the horse started to
slip on loose rocks. I was really wishing I had a horse of my own to ride.

"Do you know where to find this man?" I called back.

"I think so."

"Is Mississippi a big place?"

"Miss Emily, where we are headed is bigger than you can ever imagine. We
are headed West! And they say it's bigger than the sky itself."

I did not have any idea of what he spoke about. Big. Small. Far. Near. I had
only known one place my whole life until Pa put me on John Boy's horse
and that place was Fayette in Alabama.

"I think I will go my own way when we get there," I said.

The horse became more steady and sure-footed as it plodded down the
mountain trail.

"With all due respect, Miss Emily," John Boy called back to me. "I cannot allow that."

"And why not, may I ask?"

"I promised your pa I would look after you and take care of you."

"And so you have, sir."

"Young women cannot go off on their own."

"I don't see why not. I can hire myself out to cook and clean. I certainly know all about that," I said. "And I can take care of children, too."

"In the name of God, Emily Lowrey, I will not allow you to do so."

"Stop this horse right now," I said.

"No. We need to get to Cotton Gin Port before dark."

"Fine. When we get there, Mr. Ray, I will go my own way."

"No you won't," he said.

"Yes I will!" I yelled back. "You don't own me!"

John Boy jerked the reins so hard the horse nearly threw us both off before it stopped. He slid off the saddle and grabbed my arm and pulled me off behind him. Then he threw the reins over a tree limb and dragged me a few feet back up the trail.

"Let go of me!" I cried.

John Boy stopped and put his hands on my shoulders. "Miss Emily, listen to me."

I tried not to look at him.

"You have got to listen to me."

I stared directly at him. "Why?"

"I promised your pa I would take care of you."

"Yes I know. And you have, so..."

"Now hear me out. I also promised him I would marry you as soon as we got to a place where there was a preacher."

I stared at him even harder.

"But I do not want to get married."

"It is not up to you. It is God's will that your father gave you to me to be my lawful wedded wife."

I tried hard not to cry but the tears came hard and fast.

"Miss Emily, I was not looking to get married when I rode into your pa's blacksmith shop. I was on my way somewhere else. I had plans. Still do. Only now…you are part of them."

I kept crying.

"I gave him my word. Here," John Boy said, handing me his handkerchief.

"Besides," he continued, "a woman cannot go it alone in this world. You would either be an old spinster living by yourself in a boardinghouse somewhere or the other kind of woman that all men like to use but no man will marry."

"I do not understand," I said.

"I know," he said. "That is why I am going to marry you and give you a good, God-fearing life you could never have on your own."

I stood there.

The pine trees stood there.

Tall, proud, richly green.

But still reaching towards the endless blue sky.

"No!" I cried, and started to run.

John Boy caught me by my skirt. I fell and he stumbled and fell on top of me.

"Emily, do not fight me!"

"No! I will not marry you! No no no!"

We wrestled back and forth on the ground until he had himself back on top of me.

"It is not God I fear, sir!"

"You will be mine!" he cried. And with that, he pulled up my skirt.

I slapped at his head with both hands but it did no good. I was no match for him, he being twice my size. He slapped my face hard and fought with me until I finally gave up and just laid there.

And then it was over.

John Boy rolled off me, breathing hard.

I stared at the blue sky for the longest time without moving.

"Are you alright?" he asked as he stood pulling up his pants.

"No."

"I am sorry," he said. "I did not mean for that to happen."

"Forget it," I snapped back.

"I mean to say, well...I knew you had to be a virgin and now...I just don't know what came over me...you went wild and I lost all sense...and now I have taken that from you."

I kept lying there on the ground, staring up at the clear, blue sky.

"I am truly sorry, Miss Emily," John Boy said. "I will make it up to you, I promise. As God is my witness."

"God witnessed you just now, sir."

John Boy dropped on his knees beside me. "Forgive me."

The sky stared back at me.

He bowed his head. "Oh God, please forgive me."

I closed my eyes but the tears managed to squeeze past my eyelids and through my eyelashes and run down both sides of my face.

"Our Father, who art in Heaven," I began saying softly to myself, "Hallowed be thy name. Thy kingdom come, Thy will be done, on earth as it is in Heaven. Give us this day our daily bread."

"And forgive us our trespasses," John Boy earnestly said.

I opened my eyes and looked at him. He took my hand in both of his.

"Please?" he asked. "Forgive me my trespass."

My tears had stopped and I could see the sky was still blue.

"As we forgive those who trespass against us," I said slowly.

"And lead us not into temptation," he continued, "but deliver us from evil."

"For thine is the Kingdom," I said, "and the Power, and the Glory, forever and ever."

"Amen," he said.

"Amen," I sighed.

John Boy helped me to my feet.

"There is blood on my slip," I said.

"I will buy you a new one."

"Let us not speak of this ever again, sir,"

"You have my word, Miss Emily."

I straightened myself up while John Boy fetched the horse. I could barely walk.

"Here, take some water," he said, handing me the canteen.

I drank nearly half of it and handed it back.

"Let me help you," John Boy said as he lifted me up onto the horse.

I nearly screamed with pain but did not let out one sound. I promised myself then and there I would never cry again, ever.

John Boy got in the saddle and took the reins.

I held on lightly to his coat as we continued our descent.

5

I admire the formal dining table set for seven, although we are a
family of eight. I usually hold the baby on my lap. An embroidered
tablecloth and napkins are placed all around the table.

I believe Sunday dinners call for the family to be together in the
presence of God, and enjoy His bountiful blessings. As usual, we'll
have chicken pot pie, corn pudding, biscuits and butter, stewed
apples, green pea salad, sweet tea, and pecan pie for dessert.

Matilda comes in and stands beside me.

"Where are the boys? I told them to stay near."

"I don't know, Mama. Do you want me to go look for them?"

"No, you stay put. I need you to help get dinner ready."

Matilda is the oldest of six children I have borne thus far for John Boy
Ray. She's a good, strong girl. Especially for eleven years old. I
need her help more and more with the others. Patterson McNeal
is second oldest. My first son. He's nine and Leonard is seven and
does everything Patterson does. Or tries to, anyway.

Then there's Mary H, my fourth child. She's five and not much help. I
have two girls after her. Gincy is three and Miranda is just one year
old. But that Mary Hazelton...so defiant.

It's been a month, but it feels like yesterday.

—·—

"Mary H!" I called, but I got no reply. Then I heard the back door slam.

Yes, Mama?" Mary H answered, breathlessly.

"Look at you! Covered in dirt. What have you been doing with yourself? Dinner will be ready soon."

"I was searching for sarsaparilla root."

"You been down there visiting with old colored Bee again, haven't you?" Mary H just shrugged.

"All you do is waste time in those woods and never give one ounce of help around here. Well, never mind that now. I need you to pay attention to what I'm about to say."

"Yes, Mama."

"Patterson and Leonard are off playing somewhere. I rang the dinner bell but they must not of heard it. They don't know it's nearly time to eat, even though the sun's going down. Do you think you can go find them?"

"Yes, Mama!" Mary H cried and ran out the back door. She let it slam behind her, again, a habit I detest. I've told her a hundred times we don't live in a barn.

I looked at Matilda. "That child is wild. Maybe I should have sent you."

"Mary H will be fine, Mama. The boys are probably down at the creek whooping it up and didn't hear the bell."

"Maybe so, Matilda. Go ahead and put the potpies in the oven. You best fetch some more wood for the stove, too. Gincy, you stay put in that chair and mind your sister."

I picked up the baby and stepped outside. "Look, Miranda. There's Papa down at the barn. Wave to him." I moved her little hand up and down but John Boy didn't see us. He was too busy feeding the horses, chickens, and pigs. And our herd of Pineywoods cows.

From November, clear through winter, we will rarely sit down to Sunday dinner before dark. The days are so short. And with John Boy preaching at the Baptist church. So many of the congregation come up to him after services, seeking guidance, special prayers, a helpful hand, and even money, that he can never get away before noon. In addition, we own the grist mill and the general store so there's never a dull moment.

Nor is there enough time in the day.

I pulled the baby into my bosom and called out, "John Boy!" I waved my arm.

He glanced up and waved back.

"Dinner will be ready soon!"

He nodded and went back inside the barn.

I am still in awe of our farm carved out of a pine forest. The pine trees
tower above like protectors. They give us shelter, wood for our fires,
and shade in the hot summers. But that Sunday all I could wonder was,
Where can those boys be? Where is Mary H? It was too dark to see
beyond the barn, and the only sound I heard was Gincy crying inside.

"What is it, Gincy?" I asked, returning to the warm kitchen. "Here, Matilda.
Take the baby." I picked Gincy up and held her to me. She stopped
crying. "Did you take out the corn pudding?"

"Yes, Mama. And I'll put the pecan pie in just as soon as we sit down to eat."

"Bless you, child. I don't know what I would do without you. You are my angel."

"Oh, Mama!" Matilda grinned at me and said, "I'll go change Miranda."

Matilda left the room with the baby. I put on a pot of water to boil for
coffee. John Boy likes his pie with coffee.

"Mama! Papa!" The screams filled the barnyard. "Mama! Papa!"

I still had Gincy in my arms and rushed outside with her. Leonard outran
Mary H yelling as loud as he could. Mary H fell to the ground and
just laid there like she was dead.

"What's happened? Get up out of that mud, girl!" I cried.

John Boy came out of the barn in a panic. "What's wrong?"

"Mama! Papa! It's Patterson. I think he broke his leg. He can't move,"
Leonard screamed.

Mary H stood up and started crying.

"Hush up! You're no help!" I snapped. "Where is he, Leonard?"

"Down at the creek."

I looked at John Boy who was already hitching up the wagon.

"Get in, son."

Leonard did as told.

"Show me where."

They took off in a hurry.

"Mary H, get yourself inside this minute."

"I found them, Mama," she said.

"When? An hour ago? You probably wandered in the woods first, didn't you? Oh, my dear boy! Please God, let him be alright."

The sun had disappeared now and a heavy chill set in. I went back inside with Gincy. Mary H followed. Matilda stood at the stove, keeping an eye on dinner. The kitchen warmth belied any worries or problems.

"Gincy, you stand here next to Matilda and hold onto her apron." I glanced over at the corner of the room near the stove and saw the baby on her thick quilt with the kitchen chairs pulled around to block her in.

"Thank you, Matilda for seeing to Miranda," I said as I checked all the food.

"Where are the boys?" Matilda asked, looking at Mary H.

"You didn't hear Leonard screaming? He went with your daddy to fetch Patterson. Leonard said he broke his leg. They're down at the creek."

"Oh no!"

"Mary H, don't just stand there like a statue. Go wash your hands and face. Never mind changing your dress. You'll just get food on it anyway."

She obeyed me and left the room without a word.

"That girl will be the death of me. Gincy, go sit by the baby now. Matilda, we better set the pot pies aside and put the white towels over them. Oh, I do wish your father would hurry back."

"Don't worry, Mama," Matilda said as though she knew what was best and I didn't.

I started to correct her. I don't like young girls who put on airs. But she has been working so hard helping with the cooking and the young ones.

"You are my dearest daughter," I said and gave her a quick hug.

"What about me, Mama?" Mary H stood at the back door. I hadn't heard her come back in the kitchen.

"You look clean enough," I said.

"May I wait for Papa outside?"

"I suppose so. Put your coat on. And do not go off into those woods. Do you hear me? Or I will take a switch to you."

"Yes, Mama." Mary H grabbed her coat off the peg by the door and
    ran out.

"That child," I sighed. "What can be keeping them?"

"Should I put the pecan pie in the oven, Mama?"

"Might as well since we've got the fire going good."

I moved the kitchen chairs back around the table and picked up Miranda.

"You hungry, baby girl?"

Miranda just gurgled.

"I'm hungry, Mama," Gincy said.

"I know, Little One. Sit yourself down here by me and we'll get you some
    dinner. Go ahead and break into one of those pot pies, Matilda."

Matilda fixed a plate for her sister while I nursed the baby.

"Mama, don't you want to eat something?"

"I'm alright. Mary H is probably hungry though."

Matilda went outside to fetch her. I sat there rocking the baby in my
    arms while she suckled long and hard. Gincy ate quietly beside me.
    Sounds of the fire reminded me the pie was in the oven. I suddenly
    felt sick to my stomach. Something is wrong. John Boy should be
    back by now, was all I could think.

The back door opened and Matilda came in dragging Mary H by the hand.

"She didn't want to come in," Matilda said, exasperated.

"Sit down and eat, Mary H," I ordered.

Matilda fixed another plate of food while Mary H pulled up a chair on the
    other side of the table.

"Take your coat off," I said. "For goodness sakes, you'd think you were a
    lumberjack just come in from falling trees or something."

Mary H removed her coat and left it stuffed between her and the back of
    the chair. Matilda set the plate of food in front of her.

"What do you say?" I asked.

"Thank you," Mary H replied.

That pie must be ready, Matilda."

"Mama, I forgot all about it!"

"It's alright. Just get it out of the oven."

Matilda removed the pie. The edges of the crust were burned and the
pecans scattered on top were black as coals. She started crying.

"Now, now," I said. "It's just a pie. I promise your daddy will eat it just as it is.
Don't worry yourself about it."

Matilda dried her tears with her apron. "I'm hungry, Mama. Is it alright if I eat?"

"Go right ahead."

Matilda sat down with a plate of food. The smell of it made me feel even sicker.

"Let's pray first," I said.

We all held hands, forming a little circle around the table. "Heavenly Father,
we give thanks for this food you have provided to nourish our bodies
and souls and strengthen our faith. And thanks for the fire that warms
us this cold damp night. In Jesus' name we pray. Amen."

"Amen."

"Amen."

"Amen," whispered Mary H.

I watched the girls eat while the baby finished nursing. "It feels like hours
and hours have passed," I said to no one in particular.

I swaddled the baby and put her in the corner near the fire. She fell
asleep instantly.

"Mary H, put the chairs around Miranda."

"Mama?" she asked.

"Don't sass me. Just do it."

Gincy had fallen asleep with her head on the table. Matilda quietly removed
all the dishes. "Just let her be," I said.

Mary H dragged the chairs over by Miranda. "Mama?" she asked again.

"What?" I snapped.

"When's Papa coming home?"

"I don't know, Mary H. Maybe he and the boys would have been home long
ago if you hadn't lollygagged in the woods like you did."

I do know where they are, I told myself. John Boy went straight into town to
the doctor. That means the broken leg was something we couldn't set
ourselves. Or, God forbid, something worse.

"Matilda, we might as well bring in everything from the dining room. Mary H, you help your sister. And don't drop anything or break anything, you hear me?"

"Yes, Mama," Mary H said quietly.

The two worked at putting up the food and the unused dishes. I took another quilt and put it over Gincy and laid her down in the corner beside the baby.

"Our Father, who art in Heaven," I whispered as I started scrubbing the skillet. "Hallowed be Thy name. Thy Kingdom come. Thy Will be done. On earth, as it is in Heaven." I started to choke up. "Thy Will be done. Thy Will be done. Thy Will be done. Emily Lowery Ray, you must not cry."

Matilda and Mary H finished clearing off the dining table.

"You both need to go to bed. It's late," I said.

"Please, Mama. Let us wait up for Papa and the boys," Matilda pleaded.

"Please, Mama?" Mary H chimed in.

"Very well," I sighed. "Go get the big quilt and you two can curl up in the corner with your sisters."

It took all of five minutes and both of them were sound asleep, too.

As I washed the dishes I listened hard for the wagon wheels creaking on the dirt road. I tried a bite of pot pie and spit it out. John Boy will be starving. So will Patterson and Leonard. Maybe I should take some sasparilla tea to settle my stomach. The fire spit and crackled. All four girls slept in a pile like a litter of new pups.

I woke with a start at the sound of wagon wheels clicking loudly on the dirt road.

Wheels! It's them! I thought to myself. I can hear them coming down the road. Closer and closer.

I glanced over at the girls. All four were still in a pile fast asleep. Quietly I added wood to the fire, grabbed my shawl, and slipped outside.

Here comes the wagon around the bend. I can see John Boy. And there's Leonard beside him. Patterson is no doubt lying down in the back of the wagon. I shall wait here on the steps for him to pull the wagon up close and we can carry my dear boy inside.

John Boy drove straight to the barn without looking at me. Leonard lingered there with him while he unhitched the horse and put him in the stall with some hay and water.

The late night chill gnawed on me. I felt sick to my stomach as I watched the two of them walk towards the house. In spite of the cold, they seemed to walk slower than normal. John Boy saw me waiting on the steps and dropped his head.

"No!" I heard myself cry.

Leonard suddenly ran past me and into the house.

"No! John Boy, tell me Patterson is alright!"

My husband pulled me close to him. "Emily, our son is dead."

"Oh, dear God, no!" I screamed and fought against John Boy to let me go. He held me tight while I beat my fists against him.

"Our beloved son has gone to be with our Lord. There is nothing we can do now but pray," John Boy said, choking back tears.

"I want him back," I sobbed. "He's only nine years old! Why must he leave us now? Why?"

Tears raged down my face. John Boy dabbed at them with his handkerchief.

"The Lord works in mysterious ways, Emily."

The back door opened. Matilda stood there holding baby Miranda.

"Mama, where's Patterson?"

I started crying again.

Mary H appeared beside her.

"I want to see Patterson!" she cried.

"Get back inside!" I snapped. "You'll catch your death of cold."

John Boy and I went in behind them.

"I'll take the baby, Matilda. You go check on Leonard. He must be awfully hungry."

John Boy hung his hat and coat on the rack and sat down slowly at the kitchen table. Gincy still slept soundly on the quilts in the corner. Mary H tried to climb onto John Boy's lap.

"Leave your father be," I ordered.

"It's alright, Emily," he said.

"You need to eat something," I replied.

Mary H settled on her father's lap and gave me a look of defiance I
    would have slapped off her face if it had been any other time but
    now. Instead, I sat down at the table and started nursing the baby.
Matilda came back into the kitchen. "Leonard says he ain't hungry, Mama."
"Isn't," I corrected her.
"I know that, but he said 'ain't.'"
"Then kindly fix your father a plate of food and then it's off to bed for all
    of you."
I gave Mary H a stern look, which she clearly understood.
Matilda did as asked and placed the food in front of her father.
"Papa? Is Patterson coming home?" she asked.
John Boy shook his head.
"Why not, Papa?" asked Mary H.
"He's in Heaven now," said John Boy who bowed his head in prayer.
    "Oh mighty God, whose wonders and blessings never cease, who
    bestows upon us life, and life everlasting, O Lord who giveth and
    taketh away, we are here now offering our souls in service to you,
    and giving thanks for the nine years we had Patterson McNeal Ray.
    May he rest in peace. In Jesus' name we pray. Amen."
Matilda's eyes filled with tears.
"Now to bed," I said firmly.
Matilda got Gincy up and led her by the hand. Mary H slid off John
    Boy's lap.
"Goodnight, Papa," Mary H said. "Don't worry. Patterson can be an
    angel now."
He kissed her forehead.
"Goodnight, Mama," she then said to me.
I leaned over so she could kiss my cheek.
"He already was an angel, Mary H. And don't you forget that."
"Goodnight, Papa," said Matilda and kissed him on the cheek. She then
    did the same to me.
"Goodnight, Matilda," I said. I watched the three of them wander down the
    hall to their room.

John Boy finished his food.

"I'll make you some coffee," I said and placed Miranda in his arms.

He rocked her ever so slowly while I went to the stove.

I need to do something simple. Something ordinary. Something so everyday normal to prove that everything is the same. Nothing has changed. Patterson is asleep in his bed. I will stoke the fire. I will boil the coffee. I will never be the same again, ever.

"Snake bite," John Boy said bluntly, answering the question I'd been unable to ask.

I sat down and stared at him.

"Patterson was bit by a cottonmouth. Doc said he probably didn't know it right away. You know how those boys jump and climb and splash around in that creek. He probably thought he gouged himself on a sharp rock and just kept on playing. And then it was too late. He'd gone into shock. He'd lost a lot of blood, too."

"He'd be alive if Mary H hadn't taken her own sweet time getting down to the creek," I declared.

"Emily, don't say such things."

"It's true. You don't know that little girl like I do. She's headstrong and disobeys every chance she gets."

"She's only five."

"I wish God had taken her instead of my son!" I sobbed.

"You don't mean that!" cried John Boy.

I put my head on the table and cried.

"Heavenly Father," John Boy implored, "Forgive Emily Lowery Ray for her sharp words. She knows not what she says. Her heart is broken and she lashes out in pain. I pray you bathe her in your healing grace. And restore her faith and love. Amen."

My tears ended. I wiped my face with my apron and returned to the stove. I added more wood to the fire and boiled coffee for my husband.

He sipped the hot drink while I held the baby.

In the dark bowels of the house slept Matilda, Mary H, Gincy, and Leonard. I now have five children instead of six. Five children. Not one or two. Five.

Ages one, three, five, seven, and eleven. And yet I feel completely
empty, I thought then, and still do.

"Emily, we will hold the funeral day after tomorrow. Of course burial will
be in the Doty Springs cemetery."

"Of course," I repeated without feeling.

"Everyone will want to come back here to the house. So you will need to
prepare plenty of food. I'm sure there will be many who will lend a
hand, of course."

"Of course," I repeated.

"Let's turn in now," he said.

"Yes, of course," I said.

I banked the fire with more wood and turned down the damper for the night.

John Boy poured cold water from the pitcher into the basin and slowly
immersed his sad, tired face in the water.

I turned down the kerosene lamps while he dried himself. And then
slowly, heavily, I followed my husband down the dark hall.

"I need to check on Leonard," I said, putting baby Miranda in his arms.

I continued down the hall to the boys' room. Only now there was only
one boy.

"Leonard?" I whispered as I entered.

One bed held nothing but emptiness. The other had my sleeping son in it.

"Mama?" a soft voice said.

I sat down on the edge of the bed and took him into my arms. Leonard
cried and cried.

"I'm sorry, Mama. I didn't know. I'm sorry," he said.

"Shhh. It's not your fault, Leonard. It was an accident. And now it's all over."
I held him until he fell asleep.

And then I crawled into Patterson's narrow bed and lay there till
daybreak, vowing to never cry again.

Mary H

6

So what do you want to know?

There's not much to tell about me.

I'm nobody, really.

Just a mother and wife.

Also a daughter and sister and aunt and niece.

I am Mary.

Mary Hazeltine Ray Steed.

Everybody calls me Mary H.

Folks come to me from miles around begging and crying and pleading
    and praying for me to fix them.

I am not a magician.

I'm no witchdoctor.

And I'm no witch. Though some might say different.

I do know ways to cure certain people of certain things.

And so word has spread.

I have no private time to myself because the Good Lord has seen to it to
    give me this gift.

He has also seen to it to give me eleven children through holy wedlock
    with Newton Marshall Steed.

We married right here in Attala County, Mississippi in 1865.

I was eighteen.

We married in the Doty Springs Baptist Church where my daddy's been preaching for nearly fifty years.

All fourteen of us Ray children were born here, baptized here, married here, and some of us are already buried here.

My precious Pearly B didn't live but five months. She was my tenth child. The last daughter.

She had the prettiest eyes and fine, fine hair.

That was a bad year then.

We were all worn out.

I'd had Clevy just a year before and never got back my strength from giving birth to her when along came little Pearly.

She arrived hungry and fussy.

My milk would not go to that child no matter what I did.

Here I was, She Who Cures All, and I could not help my own little baby.

Those were dark days and also one of our coldest winters we'd had in a long time.

Pearly B came in October and together we suffered through till March when the sun began to win out over the damp chill.

But by then it was too late.

Pearly B never did improve.

For five long months her little flame would flicker or almost go out but it never did burn strong and bright. Never.

We put her in the ground on March 22, 1886.

Everybody came to the burial.

I knew it wasn't easy for Mother to watch another young'un go under.

One of my brothers died when I was five years old.

Patterson McNeal got bit by a snake.

Patterson was second to the oldest of us children but, more importantly, he was the first boy. Mother and Daddy's first son.

I think there was a lot of pressure on Leonard after Patterson died.

Leonard was only seven then and suddenly he became the oldest boy.

There were already four of us girls.

Matilda was the oldest, the firstborn.

Then I came after Leonard.

Then Gincy Abegill.

And then Miranda Brown.

A little over a year after they buried Patterson, Mother had Jelanor Victoria.

The new baby took her mind off the death of her son, and life went on.

The folks got two more sons after that.

Lawson VanBuren and then Marshall.

So Leonard finally had brothers again.

Except by then, he was eleven so the two little boys played more with
    each other as they growed.

As for us girls, it was just two more babies we had to look after.

I was fourteen when Mother had my sister, Narsis.

She as much as handed her over to me and said, "Here, you raise her."

It wasn't from lack of love or wanting.

Mother thought I needed the training.

Even though I helped with the other children over the years, Mother felt
    it was now time to prepare me to be a mother myself.

There was no discussion about it.

That's what a daughter was expected to do.

By giving me Narsis, you might say Mother never quite formed an
    attachment to her.

I don't know if she had a premonition or what.

But it's like Mother knew she was going to need her whole heart and all
    her wits about her for what would happen to her next child.

Willard arrived less than two years after Narsis. Another boy.

And of course Daddy was happy to have another son.

Something about that boy took hold of Mother.

And Daddy, too.

Maybe because he looked so much like Patterson.

Even had some of the same ways of talking and eating.

They spoiled that boy.

Oh my, did they spoil him.

Leonard was pretty much striking out on his own at eighteen when little

Willard entered the picture.

Maybe that had something to do with it.

The folks sure did cling to that baby boy.

I stood there watching Pearly B's tiny little coffin go into the small hole they
dug so nice and neat for her.

No rocks or twigs. Just smooth, wet, brown dirt.

I knew Mother was grieving more for Willard at that moment than for her
infant granddaughter or even for her first son.

It's bad enough burying one dead child, I can tell you that for sure.

But two or more is like burning to death slowly inside your heart.

Little Willard was only six years old when we lost him.

Everyone adored him.

And he never got ugly to nobody even with being so spoiled and all.

But one day he went to playing with some other boys in the cottonseed
house near town.

I suppose they were jumping and climbing on the piles of seed.

Well anyway, Willard fell down into a pile and it just sucked him in.

Nobody could dig fast enough to save him.

And all those cottonseeds just closed in on top of him and smothered the
boy to death.

We all thought for sure Mother would lose the baby she was carrying at
the time.

She was barely three months along.

But you don't know my mother, Emily Lowrey Ray.

Her faith and acceptance that all is God's Will carried her through the
death and loss and grief to bear her fourteenth and final child the
following spring.

They christened him John Pinkard but we all called him Pink from the start.

By then, I was with child. My third.

I named her Missouri Lee.

So Mother and me both had new babies at the same time that year.

It was 1870.

But Pink would be her last one at age forty-six.
Before Pink, Mother had Eudora in 1865.
And I had my firstborn in 1866. A son we call Fate, short for Lafayette.
Mother gave birth to another son, Vines, in 1867.
I had my second in 1868. A girl we call Vert.
You'd a thought Mother and me were having a contest or something.
And I won't even bother to mention my sisters and their babies.

When the Good Lord took Pearly B, I figured He was finished with me, too.
After all, I already have nine other children.
Some of them still need taking care of.
Plus my husband.
Plus my work tending to sick folk that come from all around.
I can't turn them away.
They pay what they can, or bring a chicken or pig.
And we can use whatever comes our way, being but farmers ourselves.
Now here I am.
And my youngest is dead.
Dead before she ever had a chance to live.
My oldest is already married.
Fate took Ollie Ann Ray, his second cousin, to be his wife.
Vert has Matt Bornie and they was to be wed but when this happened
     they put it off a spell.
Missouri Lee…well, she is sixteen going on thirty-two.
Rhoda Florence is fourteen.
She was supposed to take care of Pearly B like Mother had me take
     care of Narsis at that same age.
From the time I was fourteen I have had a baby on my hip.
But Rhoda couldn't take care of a sick cat much less a child.
That girl vexes me no end.
She can't cook.
She can't sew.

She should have been a boy.

All she wants is to be outside or go fishing.

If I let her go, we have fish for supper alright.

But getting her to clean them all becomes a battle until I have to beat her
with a belt to get her to straighten up.

———·•·———

"It's Rhoda's fault that Pearly B died," I said.

Mother looked at me as they shoveled the loose dirt on top of my baby's coffin.

Tears came on strong but I fought with them till I could speak again.

"It's true," I said. "That girl bounced that baby around like she was shaking
out the bed pillows. I must have told her a thousand times not to do that.
Missouri Lee could have done a better job but she's growing up so fast
and starting to bring a boy or two around. And I sure couldn't let little
Ada care for Pearly B."

"No, you couldn't," Mother agreed. She stared at the small mound of earth in
front of us. "Where is Rhoda anyway?"

"I don't know, Mother. And frankly, I don't care right now."

All the other children walked by and laid a flower on the baby's grave.

Newton stood with Daddy near the cemetery gate.

Gincy and Matilda and Leonard and Jelano and their families all filed by.

"Come on, Mary H," Mother said. "Standing here isn't going to bring back
Pearly B."

I nodded and followed her through the cemetery to the church.

Everybody crowded inside.

There were so many of us I couldn't locate Rhoda, though I looked real hard.

She's a tall girl for her age.

Dark black hair and hard black eyes. Not brown eyes. Black.

The other four girls take after my side.

But Rhoda gets her height from the Steed side of the family. She towers
over Missouri Lee.

"Mama," Ada said, suddenly appearing beside me. "I'm tired of holding Clevy."

Ada rarely complained or gave me any trouble.

"I know, Sister. Give her to me." I heaved the two-year-old onto my hip
     while Ada stood beside me, waiting.

Ada reminds me of Boot, a dog Daddy had when I was itty bitty that
     never left his side unless given an order to do so.

"Sister, have you seen Rhoda?"

"No, ma'am."

"Go look for her. When you find her, tell her to come see me this minute."

"Yes, ma'am."

I watched Ada squeeze her way between aunts and uncles and cousins
     and nephews and neighbors and disappear.

Newton sat on the far side of the room with Nando, Nolan, and Hilman,
     our three youngest boys on his lap.

I watched Hilman play with his daddy's long beard.

All the children loved doing that.

All but Rhoda.

She never did like touching or being touched.

"Mary H, you look like you could use some refreshment," Matilda said as
     she took Clevy from me and handed me a glass of tea.

I sipped it.

"You'll be fine," she insisted.

I didn't say a word.

I thought of my oldest sister's life.

She was the first born and therefore the first in line to receive food at
     mealtimes and also first to get the hand-me-downs from our cousins.

Everything started with Matilda and worked down from there.

I guess I was lucky to be number four in the long list of fourteen children.

But being the second girl, I got more chores heaped on me than she ever did.

Growing up, all I heard was 'Matilda's got talent' or 'Keep her hands nice
     so she can play the piano at church' or 'Such a pretty girl, she'll go
     far one day.'

I can still feel the sting of the dishtowel Mother snapped against my
     bare legs when I stuck my tongue out at Matilda one time.

Miss Goody Two-Shoes.

Goodness, that was thirty-five years ago.

"Are you alright?" Matilda asked.

"What?" I snapped.

"You seemed lost in thought. Thinking on Pearly B I suppose."

I half-smiled to myself. If she only knew.

I set down the empty glass. "Here, let me have Clevy."

Matilda handed me the child.

"Would you mind playing something for Pearly B? " I asked.

"Of course not," Matilda replied. She seized every chance she could to
      perform and hurried over to the piano.

"Mama?" Ada tugged at my dress.

"Yes, Sister."

"I can't find Rhoda."

"That's alright. Go sit over there and hold Clevy on your lap. Don't let her down
      till I get back."

Matilda launched into playing and many joined in singing:

> *Beautiful hands at the gateway tonight,*
> *Faces all shining with radiant light;*
> *Eyes looking down from yon heavenly home,*
> *Beautiful hands they are beckoning "come."*
> *Beautiful hands, beckoning hands,*
> *Calling the dear ones to heavenly lands;*
> *Beautiful hands, beckoning hands,*
> *Beautiful, beautiful, beckoning hands.*
> *Beckoning hands of a mother whose love*
> *Sacrificed life her devotion to prove;*
> *Hands of a father to memory dear,*
> *Beckon up higher the waiting ones here.*
> *Beautiful hands of a little one, see!*
> *Baby voice calling, O mother, for thee;*
> *Rosy cheeked darling, the light of the home,*
> *Taken so early is beckoning "come."*
> *Beckoning hands of a husband, a wife,*

Watching and waiting the loved one of life;
Hands of a brother, a sister, a friend,
Out from the gateway tonight they extend.
Brightest and best of that glorious throng,
Center of all and Theme of their song;
Jesus, our Savior, the piercèd One stands,
Lovingly calling with beckoning hands.

I stepped outside and looked towards the grassy hill where Pearly B
now rested.

The sun had gone down behind the hill and all the trees stood in black
silhouette.

And so did Rhoda.

There, beside the grave.

I'll remember that scene as long as I live.

I started towards the cemetery.

"Rhoda!" I called.

She didn't move so I guess she didn't hear me.

I waited till I got right up near her.

"Rhoda?"

"Mama!" Rhoda cried, and started to bolt.

"Don't you dare take off. I have been looking all over for you. This is no
time to be worrying me. Don't just stand there. What do you have to
say for yourself?"

"I'm sorry."

"Sorry for what?"

"I don't know, Mama. I guess I'm sorry for worrying you."

I grabbed her long black hair and twisted her head around until she
faced the grave.

"You take a good look at this."

"That hurts, Mama."

"Hush up. You never think about nobody but yourself. You want to know
what hurts? Look at that grave. That little baby grave."

I fell to my knees and pulled her down with me.

"Look at it real close, Rhoda."

I shoved her face into the mound of dirt.

"This is what hurts! This right here. And you killed her. You killed her!"

Rhoda pulled away from me and ran off.

I fell on top of the grave and let all the tears just come out. Just come on out.

I don't know how much time passed.

I didn't care.

"Mary H, pull yourself together," Mother said. "Come on now, get up."

I stood up and she helped brush the dirt off my dress.

"Listen to me," Mother said. "Pearly B is with her Savior and that's all there is to it. You can't give in to this. You have other children to take care of."

"Yes, Mother."

"Now half of Attala County is in that church besides all the family. You get back in there and be strong. Lord knows they all need you what with one complaint and another."

We started walking back through the cemetery to the church. I took Mother's arm in mine. She no bigger than me. Both of us are short and wiry.

My girls are all the same except Rhoda.

There again, she getting Newton's side of the family.

Tall, big-boned.

Even got his long arms and big feet.

Not the prettiest girl in the bunch.

"Have you seen Rhoda, Mother?"

"She tore through here earlier like a bat out of you know where. I just figured she was chasing one of them boys. Or they was chasing her."

"That girl will be the death of me," I sad as we entered the church.

Ada and Clevy still sat where I had left them except both were sound asleep on Newton's lap.

"Fate and Ollie Ann left already," Newton said. "Vert was looking for you earlier. They might have gone on too."

"Mary H," Mother said. "Your daddy's got the boys and took them on to our house. I'm going with Matilda. Let us keep them a couple days. It won't be no bother."

"Alright, Mother," I said.

I sat down beside Newton and pulled Clevy into my arms holding her as
tight as I possibly could.

At least I still had a baby to suckle.

I wanted to nurse her right then and there but she slept hard.

"Have you seen Rhoda, Newton?"

"No. But I reckon she is with Missouri Lee and some of the older boys.
Don't worry yourself about them tonight. There's enough elders
around to see to it they don't get into any mischief."

"I suppose you're right."

"I think it's high time we take these two young'uns and head home ourselves."

"Yes, sir," I sighed.

I barely had energy to stand up.

Before I could, neighbors and family started filing past me and Newton,
saying their condolences for the last time.

None of us would ever speak of this again.

Out the church door they went, climbing into their horse-drawn wagons
and buggies, some of the men and boys on horseback, many folks on
foot, walking home.

Death is over with when it happens.

Mother is right.

There is no time for grieving or wishing it weren't so.

Life goes on and we got to pick up and carry on with it.

Every family in the county knows what it feels like to bury somebody they love.

It's just the way life is.

Daddy baptized Pearly B.

And he buried Pearly B.

He baptized a hundred or more babies.

And he preached over a hundred or more graves.

So why should things be any different for me?

Rhoda

7

"Patience is a virtue, Girl. And you have none of it."

If my mother told me that once, she told me a thousand times. And there she goes, telling it to me again. As though I am the only child in the household.

There are ten of us now.

I am not the oldest. I am not the youngest. I am not even the oldest girl. I'm just there in the middle.

Fate came first. He's the oldest. And he's the first son. His Christian name is Lafayette Marshall Steed. Isn't that a handsome name? It fits him, too. But we all call him Fate for short. Mother and Daddy love Fate. He can do no wrong. Ever.

Vert came next. She is the oldest girl. Her given name is Rachel Louise. It's a fancy name, but along the way everyone began calling her Vert. She is two years younger than Fate.

Then came Missouri Lee who is two years younger than Vert. I wish my name could have been something special like Missouri. I guess that's why I never minded being called Dollie. Mother treats Missouri special too.

I am the fourth child. Rhoda Florence. The third girl. Fate was six and Vert was four when I was born. Missouri Lee was two.

Mother said from the time I was born, Vert carried me around like I was her very own doll. So that's how I got my nickname. Nearly everybody calls me Dollie except Mother and Daddy. After me came Ada Bell. She is three years younger than me and still follows me everywhere.

"Look at her! Look at her! She ate-a-bell, ate-a-bell, ate-a-bell!" I sing that until she screams for Mother and then I run the other direction.

Daddy was so happy when Campbell Fernando came along. He was born three years after Ada. And like Fate, was never called his given name except if Mother was in a temper.

"I finally got another son. Four girls are enough, Mary H." That is what Daddy called Mother. Mary H. The H stands for Hazelton but Mother never explained where that name came from.

I was seven years old when Daddy said that. I stood in the hallway just outside the nursery door listening to every word.

"No more girls. Do you hear me, Wife?"

"Newton Marshal Steed," Mother sighed. When she called Daddy by his Christian name you better know she was fit to be tied. "It is in God's hands. Take it up with Him."

"Believe me, I have. Ever since Rhoda was born, I have prayed for another son. I really hoped she was going to be a boy. I felt it in my bones. And then there she was. A girl. And then came little Ada Bell. I was beginning to lose faith. But now, dear Wife, now I have Nando."

"In His perfect wisdom, God has seen to everything," Mother said. "He put Rhoda here just at the right time so she could care for Ada and Nando."

When I heard that, I jumped into the room without thinking. "What about Vert? She's the oldest girl! Or Missouri? She's older than me!"

"Rhoda Florence Steed," Mother cried. "How long have you been outside that door listening?"

I stood like a post pounded into the ground. I could not move as I watched Mother stand up, hand the baby to Daddy, walk over to me with her mouth closed tight like she does when she is mad. Her dark eyes stared into mine until I knew I was in for it. Then she slapped me hard across the face.

"You are nothing but an aggravation. That mouth of yours is going to get

you into some kind of deep trouble one day that you won't be able
to get yourself out of. And I am not going to help you. Nor is your
father. Do you understand me, girl?"

I looked to Daddy through my tears but he kept his back to me, holding
baby Nando in his arms. "Apologize to your mother, Rhoda," he said
over his shoulder.

I hated that I couldn't stop crying so I stared at the floor.

"Well?" Mother said.

"I apologize," I mumbled.

Just then Nando started crying for Mother and I ran out of the room.

The reason I remember that day so well is because the next day was
Sunday and the whole family went to church except me. I was being
punished for being smart-mouthed. So I had to stay home and
scrub all the floors with those terrible cornshuck brushes. I tried
reminding Mother it was a holy day and supposed to be a day of
rest. In response, she said I could do all the wash too.

Mother and Daddy and the baby and the young'uns rode slowly off in
the wagon. The others skipped or walked along beside it. When
they disappeared beyond the trees, I went out to the washhouse.

I didn't mind not going to church. And I didn't mind being by myself. Truth
be told, I kind of liked it because I never get to be alone or have any
privacy to myself or anything that is just mine, all mine.

What I didn't like was all the chores Mother left for me to do. Usually Vert
and Missouri Lee had to help with some of them.

I was in the wash house scrubbing sheets up and down the washboard
when I heard a man's voice.

"Anybody home?" he called out.

I peeked out the door and saw him walk up onto our front porch. I never
had seen the likes of him before.

He knocked on the front door and called again, "Mr. Steed? You in there?"

Something about the sound of his voice scared me. I thought about
hiding, but when he started to open our front door and go in, I
stepped out of the washhouse.

"Sir!" I yelled.

He turned around. Clearly I had startled him. But he real quick-like broke into a big smile and came walking towards me.

"Hey there, young lady! And who might you be?"

"Rhoda," I mumbled.

"Is this your pa's place?"

"Yes sir."

"And is your pa Newton Marshall Steed?"

"Yes sir."

"I see," he said, looking all around. "You here all by yourself, Honey?"

"No," I lied. "My big brother's around here somewhere. Fate!" I yelled. "Fate!"

The man looked inside the wash house.

I started to take off and he grabbed my arm.

"You're lying, ain't ya?"

"Let go of me! You better let go of me!" I screamed as loud as I could.

"A little wildcat, huh!" he laughed, and dragged me inside the wash house.

"How old are you, Honey? Twelve?"

"I'm seven!" I screamed. "I'm only seven!"

"Well, you're sure a big girl for your age."

I tried biting him but he slapped me hard and threw me down on the pile of dirty clothes.

"You shut up right now, you hear?" He flicked a knife in front of my face.

That's when I smelled the liquor on his breath. I closed my eyes as tight as I could and clenched my teeth. I heard him pull his trousers down and then he was on top of me and pushing my skirt up to where it practically strangled me. I started to shake all over. When he slit my panties off with his knife I let out a cry. All I could think was how angry Mother would be that I let a perfectly good pair of panties get ruined.

"Shut up or I'll kill you," the man said. "If your pa don't wanna pay me for a day's work then I'll take my pay thisaway. And you tell anybody about this and I'll come back and kill you. And your pa."

And then he shoved himself in me and I screamed. He must have hit me. I don't know. One way or another everything went black.

When I opened my eyes, it was still light out. And the man was gone. I
   listened but I didn't hear anybody so I guessed the family was still
   at church. I tried to get up but a bad pain caught me between my
   legs. There was blood on my skirt. I crawled a little ways till I could
   stand up and then hurried to wash it out and clean myself up before
   anybody came home. I found a soft spot in the dirt floor and dug a
   hole and buried my panties.
There was no telling how much time had passed and now for sure I
   knew I would never get all the chores done much less the pile of
   wash. I started to cry and cry and I just kept on crying.
It was Mother who found me sobbing on top of the unwashed sheets.
"What in God's name is wrong with you?" she asked.
I couldn't talk. I knew she would be angry with me and disappointed that
   I hadn't done the chores and it just made me cry even more.
"Newton!" she called for my father.
Daddy came rushing into the wash house and saw me crumpled up on
   the floor crying.
"She's hysterical," my mother said, throwing up her hands.
"Now Mary H, maybe we ought not to have left her home by herself."
"I stayed alone plenty when I was her age. She is nothing but an aggrava-
   tion. I tell you the girl is worthless!" Mother stomped out the door.
Daddy bent down and lifted me into his arms. "There there, Rhoda."
I sobbed and bawled and cried as Daddy carried me all the way to the
   house and laid me on the bed I shared with Ada Bell.
He pulled the covers over me even though it wasn't a cold day, then left
   the room. Near as I can figure, something kind of went wild in me
   after that day.

When I woke up, I heard everybody in the dining room eating supper. I
   must have slept the whole day. I was so hungry my stomach hurt. I
   jumped up and a bad pain shot up through me, reminding me what
   the man had done. I also remembered that he would come back and

kill me, and Pa too, if I said anything. The pain passed and I ran to join the others.

"Rhoda-bed! Sleepyhead!" Ada Bell sang out.

"Shhh," Mother said softly. "Keep your voice down at the table. "

Ada Bell smiled at Mother and went on eating.

"About time you got yourself up out of that bed, Girl," said Mother.

I looked quickly at Pa and he winked at me.

"Sorry I slept so long," I mumbled and sat down in my chair at the table.

"You managed to miss helping with every single chore."

Vert gave me a dirty look like it was all my fault. And Missouri Lee stuck her tongue out at me when Mother wasn't looking.

"Now Mary H, she couldn't help being sickly."

Mother said not one single word to Pa.

We ate in silence for some time.

Then Pa spoke. "Mary H, you remember me telling you about that feller come worked for me the other day?"

"The stranger?"

"Yes, that would be him."

"Did he ever come back?"

"Not when I refused to pay him. He seemed down on his luck and I kinda thought he would stick around and maybe pull himself together. But he showed up in the fields smelling of whiskey. Now I don't begrudge a man a drink now and then."

"I'll say not!" Fate said, laughing.

Then Vert and Missouri Lee started laughing.

I couldn't laugh. All I could think of was this stranger Pa spoke of.

"Girls!" Mother cried.

But it was too late. One laughing made the other one laugh.

"Remember, Pa?" Fate asked.

"Yeah, Pa. Remember when Mother sent you to town?" Vert said.

"For a bolt of calico. Right, Mother?" Missouri Lee chimed in.

We all looked at Mother.

She tightened her lips.

"Yeah, that was the night you didn't begrudge a man a drink," Fate added.

"Now Fate, you be respectful to your Pa," Mother said.

Fate started laughing so hard he fell against me and I dropped my
spoon on the floor.

"Look out, Fate!" I cried.

"Rhoda! Keep your voice down," Mother scolded.

Pa just sat there grinning at Fate.

He never ever got mad at Fate.

Neither did Mother.

I stared at Pa, wishing he would get back to his story about the stranger.

"That was one long bolt of cloth, wasn't it Pa?" said Vert, laughing.

"A beautiful path of calico all the way home," laughed Missouri Lee.

Mother shot a look at Pa.

He grinned. "Now Mary H, you know it was a long hard day that day and
when I got to town there was old man Whitten. He pulled a bottle
of some mighty good whiskey out of his saddlebag and I was just
being neighborly and all."

Fate and Vert and Missouri Lee all giggled.

I kept waiting for Pa to get back to the other story.

"And it was awful dark when I set off for home. Besides, I still hold that
George Lansdale put that cloth in the back of the wagon just so it
would come all undone as I drove home."

"I never heard tell of such," Mother said with a huff.

I waited a few minutes. No one said anything.

"Pa?" I said.

"Yes, Rhoda."

"What about that man you was talking about?"

"Why on earth do you ask about that?" Mother said.

"I don't know."

"Well, Rhoda, I'll tell you, "said Pa. "He came liquored up, which is his
business. But not on my time. Even so, I let him stay. But he only
worked till dinner. And then wanted a full day's pay."

"Why would he expect that?" Mother asked.

"He wanted me to feel sorry for him, I guess. But I wasn't about to give it."

I started to choke on my food as I thought about the stranger.

Fate slapped me hard on my back. "Cough it up, Sister."

"Ouch, that hurt!" I cried.

"Hush, Rhoda," Mother demanded.

Silence once again joined us at the table.

Finally, Pa spoke again.

"I never would cheat no man, and you know that. I offered to pay him for his morning's work but he wouldn't take it. He stomped off swearing and cursing and yelling how he was going to get even."

"Goodness sakes, Newton. I sure hope he stomps his way clear out of the county."

"Oh, I think he was harmless enough. Just a lost, angry soul. He's probably stolen somebody's horse and is miles and miles from here by now."

I took a drink of water from my glass but I couldn't swallow it.

"Well, I say good riddance," Mother said. "And I say don't take on no more strangers. These are hard times for everybody and hard times make certain people dangerous."

"Still, Mary H, it's the Christian thing to do. Be our brother's keeper. Lend a helping hand and all."

"Well I say charity begins at home. You can't ever be too careful."

I couldn't hold the water in my mouth any longer and finally had to swallow. It set me off coughing.

"Rhoda Florence Steed, if I hear one more sound from you I will give you a whipping."

"Sorry," I said, in between coughs.

"And that is a promise, girl."

"Yes, ma'am."

Vert and Missouri Lee started giggling.

"Now you girls go on. Vert, you and Missouri Lee can take Nando and Ada Bell out on the porch. Let them have a little fresh air before bed."

"May I be excused, Mother?" Fate asked.

"Yes, dear."

He elbowed me in the side as he stood up.

I started to shout at him but held it all in. That's what he was trying to make me do so I would get in trouble and I wasn't going to do it.

Pa got up and went into the parlor.

Mother and I were the only ones left at the table.

"Now, Rhoda," Mother said. "Since you have had all the livelong day to rest, and you haven't lifted one finger to do a single chore around here today, you can clear off this table, put up everything, and wash and dry all the dishes and pots and pans and silverware. And be sure to wipe off the table and all the chairs and sweep the floor. And put a clean cloth back on the table for morning."

I suddenly felt very tired.

"Don't give me that look. Now get."

"Yes, ma'am."

8

Missouri stood behind me brushing my hair.

"Stop fidgeting," she said.

"I can't."

"If you don't hold still I won't be able to finish."

"Missouri Lee, go check the moon."

"I just did, Rhoda."

"Go check it again."

"If I keep going in and out, I'll sure enough wake Mama and Daddy."

"Nothing wakes Daddy," I said. "You know that."

"Maybe so. But Mama can hear a pin drop in the next county."

I started giggling.

"Hush," Missouri said as she twisted my long black hair into a braid.

"It feels like a big old heavy rope hanging down my back."

"Be still. This will keep it out of your face."

"Yes, ma'am," I said.

Missouri finished braiding my hair. She wound a red ribbon several times around the end and tied it in a bow with a knot. I jumped up.

"Think Will is here yet?" I asked.

"He better be. If you two are running off together you better hurry."

I threw my arms around my sister and squeezed her with a hug that would have to last a long, long time.

"Oh, Missouri. I couldn't have done this without you."

"I'm playing possum if anybody asks me where you went."

"Thank you. Thank you. I love Will so much."

"I know you do, Rhoda."

"It's just that I have got to get out of here or I will surely die. Look at me. I'm eighteen already and Mama is not going to stop trying to marry me off to somebody else. I want to marry Will."

"Well, look at me. I'm twenty-one and not getting any younger. At least you had a couple prospects."

"Sure I did. Old Man Passon's son with one good eye and half a brain. And John McCool who is old as Daddy. No thank you. If I don't run away now, Mama will keep me under her thumb and I will be living in her house the rest of my life taking care of her and Daddy and everybody else. I've got to go. I want my own life. And I want Will."

"So you run off and leave me here to do it all."

"Missouri, you know I don't mean for that to happen. But Mama doesn't have it in for you like she does me. She never has."

"Sister, you go. Do what you have to do. Be free. Be happy. I'm going to do the same even if I stay right here in Ethel."

We hugged again.

"Come on," Missouri whispered.

We tiptoed out of the house. The moon still hid behind the tall pine trees. I took a deep breath of the piney air.

"I hope I never see another pine tree as long as I live."

"Shhh," Missouri scolded.

The two of us held hands as we slowly walked in the dark down to the barn.

"What if he's not there, Missouri? I'll die. I'll die if I have to stay here one more day."

"He's probably keeping himself in the dark, don't you suppose?"

"I suppose," I replied.

"Will is smart. He's not going to stand in the moonlight where God and everybody else could see him."

"You're right. He is smart and I love him. He hates it here as much as I do.

Some people just don't accept him because he's from Kemper County. Especially Mama. Why in the world she is so against him I'll never know. I think it's just because he's who I want. She does it on purpose."

"I know Mama has been hard on you."

"Will wants us to go where people don't judge others by where they come from or who their folks are." I lowered my voice. "Or even what color you are."

"Is that so?"

"Yes," I said. "And Will says we have to go West to find that place."

Missouri and I reached the barn just then.

"Will?" I whispered.

"I'm here," a voice said from inside the barn.

Will walked the saddled horse out of the dark stall.

"Ready?" he asked.

"I'm ready," I replied.

Will helped me onto the horse and then he mounted in front of me.

"Missouri," I said, "There's something else I wanted to tell you."

"There was something I wanted to tell you too, Rhoda."

A door slammed in the distance. Missouri and I looked at each other.

"What was that?" Will asked.

"Best get going," Missouri said.

"Missouri! Rhoda!" Mama's voice called.

We three waited in silence. The horse started shifting and snorting.

"Newton! Newton Marshall!" Mama called. "There is somebody out there! Get your shotgun!"

"Rhoda, I'm going back," said Missouri. "I'll tell them I couldn't sleep so I took a walk."

"But Missouri…" I started to protest.

"Go! Now!" cried Missouri as she headed towards the house.

Will snapped the horse with the reins and the horse lurched ahead. "Hang on, Rho!" Will called, loud enough for all to hear.

"Rhoda, is that you?" Mama yelled.

"Rhoda! Come on back, Girl!" Daddy called.

"Shoot, Newton!" Mama cried.

"Daddy, don't shoot! It's me! Missouri Lee!" Missouri screamed from the dark.

"Shoot over there, Newton! It's Rhoda taking off with that Sistrunk boy! I knew it. I knew it."

"Mary Hazeltine Steed, I am not about to shoot my own flesh and blood!"

"Just shoot to stop her! I don't mean for you to kill her!"

I held on tight to Will as we galloped away from the barn.

Two blasts from the shotgun sounded out over the pine trees and the rising moon. I think Daddy deliberately aimed at the sky.

Their voices grew fainter as we rode.

"Give me that gun!" was the last thing I heard Mama call out.

Another blast fired but we were already deep into the pine forest and heading west.

———•—•———

The moon floated to the top of the sky as the horse picked its way through the pine trees.

We rode on this way until the moon disappeared and the early morning light began to find its way through the pines.

"Let's stop here for awhile," Will said.

He dismounted and held out his hand towards me. I slid off the horse and just as my feet touched the ground Will grabbed me.

"Come here, you wild thing," he said.

"Kiss me," I said.

We fell down on the forest floor, kissing and hugging one another, and rolling back and forth until he was on top of me.

"Right here?" I asked. "Right now?"

"Why not? There's nobody around for miles."

I started giggling as he began undressing me and himself both. "Come here, Rho."

I closed my eyes and let him take me as he had so many times before.

"I love you, Will."

We laid there on the pine needles and damp earth with our bodies intertwined. I didn't want to move from there or be apart from him ever again.

"Rho, wake up. We need to get going."

Will was dressed and holding the horse by its reins. The sun sat brightly on top of the pine trees shining down into my eyes.

I stood up and immediately felt dizzy and sick to my stomach. "Will, I don't feel so good."

"What's wrong?"

I waited forever to answer him. "You're going to have to marry me, Will."

"Why?"

"Because I am carrying your child."

"Why didn't you tell me this before?"

"You sound angry."

"I better take you back home."

"No!" I yelled.

"Rho, you can't travel on horseback in your condition."

"I don't care. I don't want the baby anyway. I just want you."

"Don't talk like that."

"It's true."

"Well, there's not much we can do about it now, is there?"

"I'm not going back there, Will. And that's final."

Will stomped back and forth in front of me, pulling the horse behind him.

I started giggling.

"What's so funny?" he cried.

"You. And that horse you're dragging behind you."

"It's no laughing matter, Rho."

"You're right. I'm sorry. So what are we going to do?"

Will stopped pacing. "I don't know," he said. "We can't stay here. The day's already getting long."

"I can walk beside you and the horse," I said.

"Are you certain?"

"I'm willing to try. I'll do anything to get out of Attala County."

"Let's keep heading west then," said Will. "Maybe we can get into the next county by nightfall."

Will and the horse went on ahead at a slow gait. I followed for about twelve

steps and knew I would never make it. My stomach turned sour
and I fell to the ground heaving with morning sickness. I knew from
being around Mama and all the babies she had after me that this
would not pass in one day or one week or even one month.

"Will!"

He jerked the horse to a halt and looked back. There I was on the
ground and feeling weaker by the minute.

"Rho! What's wrong?"

"You were right. I can't make it, Will. I'm sorry."

And then I started sobbing and shaking so much I could not stop. Will
joined me on the ground and put his arm around me.

"I'm sorry. I'm sorry," I blubbered.

"Rho, you have to think of little Willie in there," he grinned.

"Oh Will, I love you!"

"Let's get you back on the horse."

"Where will we go?" I dried my tears on my apron.

"Over to Kosciusko. We can stay with Thomas and his wife."

"Are you sure?"

"I think it will be fine for a little while."

"I guess we'll never get out of Attala County," I said.

"We will, Rho. After little Willie gets here."

"That won't be till spring."

"It's almost October now. It's not that far off," Will said.

"I need to get word to Missouri Lee."

"When we get to Kosciusko, Rho. Now let's get."

Will shoved me up onto the back of the horse and then mounted in front
of me. He snapped the reins and the horse started off.

"I'm scared, Will. All of a sudden I'm so scared."

"Maybe you should go back to your folks."

"Heavens no! They will shoot you. And me too, probably. Let's go on to
your brother's place. I hope his wife doesn't mind too much."

I held on tight to Will as we wove our way through the pines to Kosciusko.

Thomas lived on the edge of town. As soon as we came out of the pines we were at his doorstep.

"Wait here," Will said. He got off the horse and went up the porch steps to the front door.

"Hello!" he called as he knocked on the door.

I could see a light inside coming closer to the front door. Thomas's wife opened the door and thrust the burning candle towards Will.

"Who's there?" she demanded.

"It's Will. Thomas's brother."

"Thomas ain't here."

"Would it be alright if we came in and rested? We have been traveling all day."

"Who else you got out there?" She waved the candle at the darkness.

"A friend," Will stammered. "My fiancée. She's feeling poorly."

"I don't know what kind of trouble you're in but I don't want no part of it. You Sistrunks are all alike."

"We just need a place to stay the night."

"I told you Thomas ain't here."

"He won't mind," Will said.

"Go on now. Find somewhere in town to stay."

"Will!" I called. "Let's go now."

Will stomped down the steps, jumped on the horse, and we headed off towards town. I looked back and could see the candle still flickering on the dark porch.

"I never did like her," Will muttered.

"She's probably scared, is all."

"Never could figure out why Thomas married her."

"Is that what people are going to say about you?"

"They'll wonder why you married me," he replied. "All people do is talk about things that are none of their business. Besides, we're going West."

I hugged him tighter. "Yes, I said. "West. We are going West."

"But first we need to get settled for the night. If we stay at the hotel it will take most of my money, Rho."

"We can go to my sister's," I said.

"You certain of that?"

"It is our only choice. Plus Vert can get word to Missouri Lee for me without Mama knowing."

"She'll do that?"

"I'm hoping so," I said. "Go down past the church and then cross the creek. She and Matt live just past there."

The Bornie house looked cheery and bright compared to Thomas Sistrunk's place. I slid myself off the horse and nearly ran to the door. Will stayed by the horse holding its reins.

"Vert!" I knocked several times.

Finally the door flew open. "Rhoda Florence Steed, what in the world are you doing here at this time of night?" Vert cried. "Is something wrong? Is it Mama or Daddy? Who died? Is somebody sick?"

"Vert, Vert! Everything is fine. I promise you. Everybody is fine."

"You scared me half to death, Sister. Get yourself in here."

"Wait, Vert. I'm not alone." I turned and motioned for Will to come ahead.

"Is that Will Sistrunk?"

"Yes, ma'am." I could not keep myself from smiling.

Will tied the horse and walked slowly up the porch steps. "Evening, ma'am," he said, tipping his hat.

Vert looked at his suspiciously. "Evening, Will. You can take your horse down to the barn. There's water and feed there. Help yourself. Matt is down there. He can show you."

"Thank you, ma'am."

Will left as Vert grabbed me by the arm and pulled me inside. "Come on in the kitchen, Sister. You can dry dishes while you explain what you're doing here at this hour of night with that young man."

"Might I just sit a spell, Vert? I'm feeling poorly."

"I thought you said nobody was sick?"

"I'm not."

"Have you eaten?"

"Nothing all day."

"Goodness sakes, Rhoda. I will fix you a plate."

"I'm not sick, Vert. I'm pregnant."

Vert dropped the wooden spoon in the pot she was stirring.

"Will and I ran off yesterday," I continued. "We are going out West. I didn't tell him about the baby because I knew he wouldn't take me. But then I got so sick this morning I just knew I couldn't make it, so here we are."

"Oh Rhoda," Vert sighed.

"Vert, I cannot go back to Ethel. I can't. I'll die. Mama is set on killing me." I started sobbing.

"There, there. Shhhh." Vert put her arm around me and I shoved my face into her apron.

"Sister, you will make yourself sicker if you keep on like this. Hush now."

I cried even harder.

"Now get your wits about you while I fix you a plate."

Vert returned to the stove and I dried my face on my own apron. I didn't know I was so hungry until she set biscuits and gravy, potatoes, and fried green tomatoes with bacon and a bowl of apple cobbler in front of me.

"Vert, is there enough left over for Will to have some?"

"Of course, Sister."

I kept on eating.

"Rhoda, you got yourself into a fine mess. People will talk. What about the Reverend and Grandmother? Oh for goodness sakes."

"As soon as I get past this morning sickness, we will leave."

"No you will not! You are staying right here until that baby comes."

"But Vert, that won't be till next spring."

"So be it. We have room."

"And what about Will?"

Vert sat and thought for several minutes while I finished eating.

"I will see Mama and Daddy in Doty Springs on Sunday, just like always," Vert said.

"Will you please tell Missouri Lee to come see me? I want to tell her about the baby myself."

"Yes, I'll give her the message. You realize everyone will be wondering where

you are. And I am going to tell them you and William Sistrunk ran off
to get married."

"But Vert!"

"Hear me out," she said, holding up her hand just like our grandfather,
the Reverend John Boy Ray, has done in church every Sunday for
the past forty years. "Your sins," she continued, "are not going to be
visited upon this family if I have anything to say about it. Your sins
are to stay between you and God. If you want my help, and if you
are going to stay in my house, then you will get married tomorrow.
Six months from now when the baby arrives, people will have
forgotten how much time has passed. Besides, babies come early
all the time. Is that clear?"

"What if Will doesn't want to marry me?"

"If he is a real man, and a good Christian, he will do the right thing and
marry you."

"I hope so," I said.

"We will find out tomorrow. Will can sleep in the barn tonight. You can sleep
with little Emily. I don't want to move her out of bed at this hour."

"Oh, Vert. I feel terrible now that I have come."

"Stop that. Tomorrow night when you are man and wife, you and Will shall
take Emily's room and Emily can sleep on the daybed in the parlor."

"I hate putting you out like this."

"Rhoda, we are family. Besides, a married couple needs their privacy if at
all possible. Now pray with me."

I closed my eyes and bowed my head. Vert held my hand as we both
spoke aloud,

"Our Father, who art in Heaven
Hallowed be thy name.
Thy kingdom come, Thy will be done
On earth as it is in Heaven.
Give us this day our daily bread,
And forgive us our trespasses
As we forgive those who trespass against us.

And lead us not into temptation,

But deliver us from evil.

For thine is the Kingdom, and the Power, and the Glory,

Forever.

Amen."

Vert squeezed my hand. "A baby! Oh Rhoda, isn't that a blessing?"

I nodded. How could I tell Vert that it was the last thing I wanted?

9

I am going to be married. I am going to have a baby. I stood in the
parlor and stared at myself in the mirror, thinking. All I wanted
was to run away with Will. All I wanted was to get out of Attala
County and be free.

"Rhoda, are you ready?" Vert suddenly appeared beside me. "Reverend
Bornie will be here any minute."

"Yes, Vert. Ready as I'll ever be."

"You look just fine. Where is the groom?"

"He stepped out back to get some air."

How can I tell her Will doesn't want this any more than I do? Will
wants to be free. He wants to go out west.

"Is he doing alright by you?"

All I could do was nod my head.

"Vert, you are telling Mama that we ran off to get married. I don't want
you to lie on account of me. Besides, won't folks find out Reverend
Bornie married us right here in Kosciusko?"

"I am not telling a lie. You ran off. Correct?"

"Yes."

"And now you are getting married. Correct?"

"Yes."

And as for the Reverend, he is a man of God and does not divulge anyone's private matters. Plus he is Matt's uncle, which is why we called on him. This remains in the family. You understand."

I felt the tears building up and fought to keep from crying.

There was a knock at the front door and Vert left to answer it. I dabbed at my eyes with my handkerchief.

"I have a surprise for you, Rhoda."

I turned around and there stood Missouri Lee.

"Sister!" We both screamed as we grabbed each other and hugged and kissed.

"I thought I would never see you again," she cried.

"Me too!"

I looked over at Vert who just smiled. "That's your wedding present from me," Vert said. "Matt sent Bunk over to Ethel at daybreak to fetch Missouri."

"What about Mama?" I asked.

"She knows I'm always running off," Missouri laughed.

Another knock sounded at the door.

"That will be Reverend Bornie," Vert said. "Now listen, you two. We are going to Doty Springs now. Missouri Lee will stand up for you as your witness."

I hugged Vert.

The knocking on the door continued.

"Coming!" Vert called and rushed out of the parlor.

Missouri and I just stared at each other in disbelief that this is how all our plotting and planning ended up.

"You look different," Missouri said.

"So do you."

"It's only been a couple days since you left. Maybe it's all this excitement but you have a glow about you. Are you excited about getting married?"

"Not really."

Missouri Lee laughed. She knew me better than anybody else in the family.

"Vert's doing, am I right?"

"Yes, ma'am."

Just then Vert returned with Reverend Bornie. "Reverend, you remember my two sisters, Missouri Lee and Rhoda Florence?"

"Yes I do," he replied. "How do you do, ladies."

We both curtsied and said, "How do you do, sir."

"Reverend, come into the kitchen and have a hot cup of tea while Rhoda and Will get prepared. Matt and Emily and I are going on to church."

Reverend Bornie and Vert left and I turned to Missouri.

"I must tell you now and tell you quick. I am carrying Will's child."

Missouri gasped.

"Yes. It's true. I wanted to tell you before we rode off but I just couldn't and then the next morning I got so ill with the morning sickness that I had to tell Will."

"You mean he didn't know either?"

"No. He would never have taken me if I had told him beforehand. And now I've ruined his plans to head out West."

"Oh Rhoda, what are you going to do?"

"I'm standing here about to get married. And I feel like crying."

"And Will?"

"He's biding his time outside. He's not too happy either. Oh Missouri, I don't want this but what could I do? Will insisted we stay put until the baby is born. And Vert insisted we be married immediately. She's telling Mama and Daddy we ran off to get married. We'll wait as long as we can before letting them know about the baby."

"We are going to Doty Springs now!" Vert called from the foyer. "Rhoda, don't keep the Reverend waiting. Go get Will!" The front door closed behind her.

Missouri and I both went to the window and looked out. Matt and Emily were in the wagon. Vert climbed in and they drove off.

I ran to the kitchen. "Reverend Bornie, would you please fetch my fiancé? He is outside somewhere and I don't want to dirty my dress."

The Reverend complied and I ran back to the parlor.

"Missouri, be quick. What is it you wanted to tell me?"

"You are in luck. Mama is not going to care one way or another about your doings."

"What? Why not?"

"I am also with child."

I gasped.

"Yes, it is true. And I am not getting married. So you can see how tongues will wag over that. I know Mama knows even though I haven't told her or anybody else. That is, until now. I wanted to tell you the other night before you rode off but it just didn't come out."

"What will you do?"

"Have it, of course."

"What about the father?"

"Rhoda, you must promise never to tell nobody, never, ever. Promise?"

"I do."

The father…oh God, I don't know if I should tell you or not?"

"Tell me. I told you my secret."

"Miles Crow."

"You mean the preacher here in Kosciusko? Pastor Crow?"

"Oh, Missouri Lee! He's a married man with five children!"

"Don't you think I know that?"

"Does he know?"

"Yes. He loves me. He wants to marry me and make it right. Now couldn't you just see that happening?"

"You would be tarred and feathered and run out of the county," I said softly.

"Exactly. So I will leave the county before I start to show. Like I said, Mama knows. She can spot a woman the day after she conceives. I have suggested to her that I go down to Jackson and find some employment to help out with the family and all. She agreed at once. See, she knows. So that's where I am headed and will stay until the baby comes. And then I will come back home."

"Just like that?"

"Yes, just like that. I have no other choice."

"Neither of us do," I sighed.

"But what Mama doesn't know is that I'm bringing my baby back with me."

"Missouri Lee!" I gasped.

We hugged each other tightly.

Will shuffled in followed by Reverend Bornie. He and I exchanged glances.

Then we stood side by side and looked at the Reverend who opened his Bible and began, "Do you, William James Sistrunk, take this woman, Rhoda Florence Steed, as your lawful wedded wife, to have and to hold..."

·Ann·

10

The photographer rode away in his wagon pulled by the biggest horse in the whole wide world. I ran inside. All the others were crowded around. I squeezed between Mama and Papa so I could see the family picture too. Never in my life had I ever seen a photograph, much less been in one.

There we all were in front of our house in Big Springs, Texas. A couple of chairs had been brought out. All us girls were in white dresses with big bows on the back of our heads. Mama's dress was white too, except it had blue flowers. But the picture was just black and white.

"What happened to the color, Mama?" I asked.

The girls giggled.

"That's just how it comes out, child."

"It's not a painting, silly," said Ruby.

"I know that," I said.

"Hush, Annie," Mama said.

So there we all were, everybody gathered on that piece of paper, staring right back at ourselves. Everybody except me.

In the picture, Mama and Papa are sitting on chairs surrounded by us kids. Blanton is standing behind them. She's the oldest and all growed up. Mama says it's high time she got married since she's nineteen-years-old and not getting any younger. Her full name is Willie Blanton Sistrunk, but everybody calls her by her middle name. Papa wanted a boy real bad and that's why she got the name Willie. Papa says he grew up with five brothers and only one sister and that's why he likes boys better. Blanton is real tall and pretty and has the blackest hair. Just like Mama's. She has it pinned up like Mama, too. Blanton lets me watch her when she fixes her hair. She brushes it and brushes sit and then she takes a comb and pulls a part through it right along the top of her head and then she brushes the hair into two parts and pulls each one down over her ears and back up and around and pins it up in the back. When she's done, it looks like she's wearing a black hat. Just like Mama.

Ruby May is behind Papa's shoulder and resting her arm on his chair. I think Papa likes her best of all the girls. She is fourteen. Ruby has dark brown hair braided into two loops. Her big bow is the same material as Mama's dress—white with little blue flowers.

Mary Thelma stands on the other side near Mama. We call her Mary T. She has her hair in braided loops like Ruby, but her big bow is dark blue. She's ten.

Jimmie Nita is in front of Ruby. Papa was still waiting for a boy when Jimmie was born. She's eight. Mama said she put her foot down when Ruby and Mary T came along. They were females and they were going to be baptized with female names, that's all there was to it. But when the fourth baby was a girl, too, Mama gave in. And Papa named her Jimmie. Her big bow is shiny green. But you'd never know it by looking at the picture.

Right next to Mama is Ole Detmer, our brother. He's five. If Papa had waited, Jimmie could have had a girl's name because Det came right after Jimmie. Mama says Papa was so happy to finally have a son.

Then came me.

My name is Annie Beatrice.

I'm the girl that came between the two boys.

I don't have black hair. Or even brown hair. Mine's white.

I don't have braids. Mine's short.

I don't have a big bow in my hair. I don't have nothing in my hair.

I'm almost four years old. I can count to a hundred and say my ABCs, too.

In the picture I'm standing next to Papa's leg and in front of Mama who had hold of the back of my dress to keep me still. I don't know how to be still. Mama keeps telling me to be still but nobody else has to be still.

Papa holds the new baby on his lap. It's the first baby I ever saw. He came out of Mama. His name is Everly James. Even he wears a long white dress because we all went to church that day to get him baptized so God will take him to heaven if he dies.

During the picture-taking Mama jerked my dress to be still but the baby made a funny sound and I looked at him just as the photographer yelled, "Hold it!"

Snap! Click! Poof! It was over. That tells you why I'm not looking straight back out like everybody else is. I'm looking at Everly.

"I think the picture came out real good," Papa says.

"Except for Annie," Mama replies.

"That girl sure doesn't look like any of us," says Papa.

"She gets that from my mother's side," Mama says, "being short, I mean."

"Yes, but she's so chubby. The child doesn't get that from my side."

"Well, mine either," says Mama. "I didn't really realize how blonde her hair is until I see her with all the rest of us."

"It's practically white. You sure she is mine?"

"William James Sistrunk! What are you implying?"

Papa laughs. "Rhoda, you have to admit I am gone for spells at a time. And it's been about four years since I started working the Galveston line."

"For heaven's sake," Mama huffs.

"Speaking of Galveston, I better get to the station."

"Don't go, Papa!" we all yell.

"Now children," says Mama.

I lean hard into Papa and wrap my arms around his arm. "I don't want you to go."

"Now Annie, don't bother your father with your whining. Blanton, get the girls ready. Annie, put your shoes on. We'll walk your father to the station."

I try to hold onto Papa's arm so he won't leave again, ever.

I'm always so happy when he comes back. One time he brought a really big seashell all pink and shiny and if you put your ear to it you can hear a sound. Papa says that's the sound of the water. Mama keeps the seashell on her dresser so I won't break it.

"Go on, Annie. Mind your mother." He pulls his arm from mine and I just stand there.

"Hurry up, child!" Mama cries, "Your father has a train to catch."

I take off running to get my shoes.

———•·•———

Six years have gone by since that photograph was taken. And I'm still running. Seems like all I do is run.

Run to catch up with my sisters, which I never do. All they do is laugh at me.

Run to get away from my brother, Det.

Run from Mama when she tries to grab hold of me. And then I run away from her after she does.

Run to Papa when he gets off the train.

Run out the door to see the funeral wagon go by with five little coffins on it. Mama said there was a little girl just like me inside one of them. So I better mind her and be good.

Run to help take the clothes off the line before it rains.

Run to feed the chickens.

Run away from the rooster.

Run to feed the hogs.

Run after the dog who took my washrag.

Run to put more wood on the fire.

Run to take the kettle off the stove.

Run to help with the babies. Mama had two more after Everly. Both are girls. Papa was not pleased. So he named the first one Jonnie True and the last one Frances, who Papa calls Frankie. And so does everybody.

Frankie and Jonnie. You'd think they were boys.

I'm always running to do this or running to do that.

Mama makes it seem like there's something wrong with me.

One time Papa laughed and said, "Rhoda, she just takes after you."

Mama stopped what she was doing and stared real hard at him.

"I recall when you were young," Papa continued, "you ran away from
   your mother."

"Are you saying I'm old, William?"

Every one of us kids looked at Papa, waiting.

"No, I didn't mean that."

"What did you mean then?"

"I was just remembering how spirited you were. Annie's got that from you."

Mama got so mad she stomped out of the room. Papa went after her
   and we could hear their voices, but we couldn't make out what they
   were saying.

Detmer gets to run in and out of the house whenever he wants and
   Everly tries to keep up with him.

The big girls pay me no mind so they can go wherever they want.

11

I'm ten now. But I'm short and fat, Mama says. That's why I'm not real fast.
   Mama makes me wash the floors while the boys and my sisters run in
   and out not caring where they step. The more I wash and scrub, the
   more they all run in and out like it's a game. Like one time...

"Annie!" Mama called from the house.

"I'm out here, Mama!" I yelled back. I was trying to pump up more water so I
   could finish the floors and Detmer kept throwing rocks at me.

"Stop it, Det! Stop it or I'll tell Mama!"

"Go ahead! I don't care!"

He threw a dirt clod against my head and it busted into a million pieces all
   over my hair.

"Now you're going to get it!" I dropped the pail of water and took off running
   after him.

Detmer ran around in circles laughing. I got dizzy trying to catch him and fell
   down. Next thing I knew I was pulled to my feet.

"What do you think you're doing?" Mama demanded.

She looked me up and down. I was covered with dirt from my head to my
   shoes. Before I could speak, she said, "You come with me right now."

Mama grabbed my arm so tight I thought it would break in two.

"But Mama, Det was throwing rocks at me."

"That's no excuse. You should pay him no mind. He's just being a boy.

Detmer, you go play now, you hear!"

"Yes, Mama!" he cried, and ran off.

Mama dragged me by the arm all the way to the house, up the steps, through the back door, and into the kitchen.

"Look at you! You're as filthy as those hogs out there. And just as dumb. Now look at this floor."

Mama twisted me around and made me look at the wet floor with all the dirt tracked across it.

"Looks like an army tromped through here. Get me the belt."

Mama let go of my arm. I looked at the belt hanging on the door. I wanted to run straight out that door but I knew she'd catch me and then I'd really get a beating. So I got the belt off the hook and handed it to her.

"What do you have to say for yourself?"

"Mama, I did wash the floor, but the big girls ran through and then Det..."

"Hush up right now. Always making excuses."

"I'm sorry, Mama."

"That's it? You're sorry? You are nothing but trouble. As if I don't have enough to worry about."

She flipped me over her knee, pulled my dress up to my waist, and snapped the leather on the back of my bare legs.

"Don't think you're too big for me to give you a licking."

I screamed in pain.

"I'll give you something to be sorry about!"

She hit my legs with the belt, again.

I screamed again.

"Be still! You already woke the babies. You're a good-for-nothing child is what you are!"

The belt stung my legs four more times but I didn't make a sound. Mama seemed to run out of steam after that.

"Now get this floor clean and don't let me hear another word out of you today. Do you understand me, Annie?"

Tears ran down my face but I kept still.

"Did you hear what I said?"

I nodded.

Mama hung the belt back on the door.

"Well, don't just stand there. Go get the pail of water and be quick about it. Your father's train will be here soon. I know he doesn't expect us to meet him at this hour so we need to hurry. I thought it would be nice to surprise him but you had to go and make trouble and now we're all late. Blanton! Girls!" she called as she left the room. "Come help me with the babies."

Papa was coming home. Oboyoboyoboy. I ran outside and got the pail of water and ran back in before Det saw me. I latched the back screen door so he would have to stay out. And then I scrubbed and scrubbed as fast as I could and I dried and dried the floor before anybody could set foot in the kitchen.

"Mama!" I called.

"What?" She stood in the doorway. "Don't yell in the house, I'm right here."

"I wanted you to see the floor all clean."

"Yes, I see."

"So can I go with you to meet Papa?"

Mama looked at every inch of floor and in every corner and under every chair.

"Please, Mama."

Finally she said, "I suppose so. But get out of those dirty clothes."

I ran out of the kitchen to change.

"And hurry it up," Mama said as she went out to the front porch.

The big girls, Ruby, Mary T and Jimmie, were all clean and dressed and sitting on the porch with little Jonnie True. Blanton sat out there too, holding baby Frankie. I could hear Detmer and Everly chasing each other around the yard. They were probably getting all dirty.

"Look at those boys," Mama laughed. "They sure know how to keep themselves occupied."

It took me no time to pull off my apron and dress and socks and put on a clean one of everything. The back of my legs burned something fierce so I took some cornstarch we keep by the baby's bed and rubbed it on my sores. I brushed my short hair once on one side, once on the other side, and ran to join the others. The screen door slammed behind me.

"Annie Beatrice Sistrunk!" cried Mama.

"Annie! For goodness sakes," Blanton scolded.

Baby Frankie started to cry.

"Now see what you've done?" said Blanton.

"I'm sorry."

She stood up and started gently bouncing Frankie in her arms to quiet her.

Mama looked at me and just shook her head and sighed.

"Come on, girls," she said, taking Jimmie and Mary T by the hand. "Let's
go meet your Papa."

Ruby followed them down the steps holding on to Jonnie True.

Blanton was behind her carrying the baby.

And then me.

The boys shot out from behind the house and ran on in front of Mama.

"Detmer, please run up ahead so we don't have to walk through all your dust."

He laughed and waved and took off with Everly scrambling behind him.

"Thank you!" Mama called to him.

I could walk to the train station with my eyes closed. At least I believed
I could. Since everybody was in front of me, I decided to try it. I
closed my eyes and kept walking as I listened to Blanton's shoes
crunching along in the dirt in front of me. It seems like I went for
quite a ways but then my foot came down on a rock and turned my
ankle enough that I fell.

Nobody saw.

Nobody looked back.

I was glad of that.

I brushed myself off and hurried to catch up but my ankle hurt some so I
couldn't go as fast as I wanted to.

By the time we got to the station, I was limping. Now I was really in for it.

Mama didn't notice because her eyes were watching for the train.

Pretty soon we heard the train whistle blow.

Detmer and Everly got so excited. They ran up and down the platform
until Mama called them back.

"Boys, please stay here with me. I don't want you falling down onto those tracks."
They came and sat down on the bench where the rest of us sat.

"Thank you," said Mama. "You are good boys. Papa will be proud of you."

The train whistle blew again as the train chug-chug-chugged into the station and screeched to a stop. It let out a real loud hissing sound and then everything got quiet and the people started getting off the train.

We all sat at one end of the platform. The engine was clear down past the other end. Papa usually got off somewhere near the engine as he was a fireman for the T & P.

Every single one of us was looking to the right, trying to be the first one to spot him. Pretty soon we saw a woman step down off the train. She turned and waited and right behind her came Papa. He put his arms around her and hugged her.

I looked over at Mama. She stood up but didn't move. Her face didn't look too happy.

The lady from the train was hugging Papa back. She was short and pretty and younger than Mama. She had on a real tight skirt that came only to her knees. And she was wearing leather boots with real high heels. Stuck in the side of one boot was a little pistol.

None of us moved as we watched her and Papa kiss each other goodbye. They kissed for a long time.

Mama turned to all of us and said, "I do not want to hear a word about this from any of you. And I don't want you telling your father we were here. Now let's go."

She picked up little Jonnie True and started walking towards home as fast as she could. Blanton ran after her, trying to keep baby Frankie from bouncing up and down. The girls all looked at each other and then at me. I looked at the boys and then at them.

"You heard what Mama said," I cried. "Get going."

They all took off like a fire had started underneath the benches.

I stayed.

And watched.

The lady and Papa were talking and laughing and I could tell they really liked

each other and were having fun. I don't think I ever saw Papa smile
so big as he did with that lady.
Then Papa turned and looked down the platform to where I was sitting.
I waved.
He waved back.
The lady watched.
I waved again.
He said something to her and then headed towards me. She walked off
in the other direction.
"Hey, Annie!"
"Papa!" I jumped up and immediately fell back down on the bench.
"What's wrong?"
"I hurt my ankle."
"Oh, Annie. It's always something with you. Is your mother here?"
"No, sir."
"Does she know you're here."
"No sir," I lied.
"Oh, Annie. You just can't stay out of trouble, can you? How long you
been sitting here?"
"Not long," I lied again. But I crossed my fingers so it wouldn't stick.
"Well, we better get on home."
I stood up but I couldn't walk.
"Hurts that bad?"
"Yessir. I'm sorry, Papa."
"Come on. I'll give you a piggyback ride home," he laughed.
I climbed on his back, forgetting about where Mama had whipped me.
Papa put his arms under my legs to hold me on his back.
"Ow, ow!" I screamed.
"What's wrong now?" he asked.
"Nothing. I'm just a little sore."
It hurt pretty bad, but I didn't care. I had Papa all to myself. I wrapped my
arms around his neck and held on tight as we headed home.
"Papa, tell me about your train ride."

"Well, there's not much to tell. We ran to Galveston and back like always. Didn't run into any weather this trip."

"Tell me about Galveston."

"Annie, I've told you about Galveston before."

"Tell me again. Please!"

"Alright," he finally said. "Galveston is an old port town on the Gulf of Mexico, which is a big, big body of water. And it's a long, long ways from Big Springs. You go south from here and when you can't go any further because the land ends and there's nothing but water, that's when you know you're in Galveston."

"How big is the water?"

"Big. Really big. You can't see the end of it."

"Like the sky?"

"Yes, something like that."

"I wish I could see it."

"Maybe one day you can, Annie."

I could have listened to him forever and ever.

"Maybe one day when I grow up?"

"Maybe so."

"When will that be, Papa?"

"Sooner than you think."

"But when is that?"

"You'll know, Annie. You'll know."

I wanted us to keep on going and never go home.

Never, ever.

12

I could kill 'em…if looks could kill, they'd all be dead…I mean it…
every one of 'em has been so mean to me…every single one…
except Frankie…she's the baby of the family and sure is spoiled…
I think Jonnie's the meanest of all…she thinks she's so high and
mighty because she's pretty…and she is pretty…prettier than any
of the rest of us Sistrunk girls…she could pass for Betty Grable
now that she's older…wears her hair the same way…and has a
real nice figure…boys flock around her like flies…every boy that is,
except Will. And she couldn't get him to fawn all over her…'cause
he loved me…

I'm sure of it or I wouldn't say so…I'm sure glad we moved from Texas to
California otherwise I never would have met William Clock. I never
would've known a boy like him in Texas because we never got to
meet anybody new there just the same old kids around all the time.
Most of 'em big families, like ours, and living hand-to-mouth or
struggling or just getting by.

But the Clocks were different than any kind of people I'd ever met
before. I knew I loved Will the minute I saw him.

Now he was what you'd call a real looker…but nice, too. He was so nice,
always polite… and gentle… and nice. I never could see why he and
my brother got along so good. Detmer, that's how I met Will Clock,

because he and Detmer worked together and one day Det brought Will
home with him to have supper with the whole family. I bet that was an
eye-opener for Will to sit down with such a crowd of people. William has
two sisters, that's it.

The Clocks own rides and booths at The Pike over there in Long Beach…
bumper cars and the booths where you try to toss a quarter on a
plate and win a goldfish or stuffed animal. They also sell his mother's
homemade pies. They own houses too, besides their very own house.
They own all that and there's just the three kids, Will, Helen, and Thelma.
Not a whole mess of kids like us Sistrunks or Mother's family of ten
children or her mother who was one of fourteen.

Mr. and Mrs. Clock are real fine people. I can't ever bring myself to call them
anything but Mister or Missus or Sir or Ma'am. I could never call 'em by
their first name, even though she told me I could call her Kittie, but I just
never could.

Will's sister Thelma never liked me, or any of the rest of us, really, and any
chance she could she would be mean. She called us "The Tribe." Thelma
always wore a fur coat or mink stole, and never thought I was good
enough for her brother. I never did either really but I couldn't wait to get
away from my family, from my mother, I never fit in with the rest of 'em
and I was ready to do anything to be free.

Some might say I tricked Will Clock but that ain't so. I was fourteen going on
fifteen and he was twenty-one. He didn't have to do anything special
to get me. I wasn't the way Jonnie got to be. She'd flirt and tease and
lead a fella on. If they wanted more, they had to pay for it by buying her
jewelry or clothes. She loved those clothes…and hats and shoes. They'd
do just about everything, take her out to supper, drive her places, and
just, I don't know, spend plenty of money on her.

Will Clock bought me an ice cream cone.

I wasn't no tramp like little Jonnie.

And I knew I wanted to be with him forever.

It's so hot.

And I'm so fat.

I am so fat.

I've always been fat. Everybody's always told me, "You're fat, Annie." I'm
the fattest one in the family. Growing up, the older girls made fun
of me. They said I was adopted and that a big ol' fat woman left me
beside the side of the road in the bar ditch where Mama found me
when the family was walking back from church.

I don't believe it now, but I sorta did back then because I do not look like
any of my sisters…or brothers. I guess that's why Mama beat me.
All I can figure is that she was ashamed of me…the Ugly Duckling.

But Will always smiled at me. Maybe he felt sorry for me; I don't know
and I don't care. They may say I'm not too bright, and I don't know, I
may be stupid like they say, but I have learned one thing…I have to
take what I can get. No one else is gonna hand me happiness on a
silver platter.

Sure, I might have played it up just a little with Will. I learned how to do
that from Jonnie. She was so effective with everyone.

So there was Will at our dinner table. Thanks to Detmer. As we passed
around the mashed potatoes and gravy, I wondered if I'd ever see
him again. So I had to think fast. And that's hard for me, with me
being fat and everybody treating me bad and like I'm stupid. But I
had to take a chance.

I don't cry.

My last tears fell in Texas.

I learned real quick not to cry or Mama would beat me again for crying.

"Don't be a bawl baby!" she'd yell.

"I wouldn't cry even if you died," I mumbled.

"Speak up, Annie. If you got something to say, you better say it to my face."

"Nothin, 'Mama."

"You are a thorn in my side, girl. And don't you forget it."

"I won't."

"Don't sass me now."

"Yes, ma'am."

Mama taught me good…that's about all she taught me…that and reading and learning the Bible. Her daddy was the preacher in the Baptist church back in Mississippi where Mama's from and all of 'em kids had to know the Bible. I always wondered why we lived in Texas when all Mama's sisters and brothers and mother and daddy were all right there together in Doty Springs. She never would say. Then we up and moved even further away to California, but I'm not complaining because that's when things got better for me. But only for awhile.

Ruby was the one taught me about how babies got made. Not Mama. Jimmie knew too, but she would just giggle when Ruby talked about a boy and a girl and what they did together when they were naked. We three girls slept in the same room. Ruby and Jimmie got the big bed and I slept in a single bed by myself. Ruby liked to talk at night when we were all in bed and it was dark.

"Does it hurt?" I asked.

"Yes, but in a good way," Ruby said.

Jimmie giggled.

"I bet Jimmie's blushing."

"Am not," Jimmie said.

"Have you done it?" I asked Ruby.

"Of course not. You're supposed to be a virgin when you get married."

"What's a virgin?"

"A girl who hasn't done it yet."

"Done what?"

"You know….It."

"Jimmie," I asked, "Do you know what she's talking about?"

Jimmie just giggled.

"Annie, listen," said Ruby. "It's called intercourse. And once you do it, you aren't a virgin anymore."

"So why do I have to be married?"

"Because it's sinful and wrong and dirty if you do it before you're married."

"Getting married makes it pure," Jimmie added.

"And beautiful," Ruby said.

"But if you do it and you ain't married, it's ugly?" I asked.

"Yes."

"What about the boy?"

"Oh, he can do what he wants," Ruby said.

"He doesn't have to be a virgin too?"

"No," they both answered.

"If he's a God-fearing man, he'll probably be one," Ruby added.

"But if he isn't a virgin, he had to do it with somebody," I said.

Ruby and Jimmie were both quiet.

"What?" I asked, "Tell me."

"Annie, you're dumber than a doorknob," Ruby said.

Jimmie got up and listened at the door. "It's all quiet out there. Guess
Mama and Daddy went to bed. Everybody's asleep." She climbed
back into bed with Ruby.

"Harlots," said Ruby.

"What?" I asked.

"Whores and harlots. Tarts. Prostitutes. Evil, sinful, bad women. They do it
for money."

"Some do it because they like it," Jimmie giggled.

"You're not supposed to like it. Not unless you're married. And even then,
it doesn't matter," Ruby said.

"You mean like that lady Daddy got off the train with that time with the
real tight skirt and the pistol in her boot?"

"Shhhhh," snapped Ruby. "Don't ever let Mama hear you say that."

"So how come you know it hurts, Ruby?"

Jimmie giggled.

"Mary T told me."

Mary T was older than all of us and got married not very long ago.

"She said it hurt the first time. She says it gets easier after that."

"So she was a virgin?" I asked.

"Of course she was, Annie! Shame on you if you think otherwise."

"I guess she'll have a baby now," I guessed.

"Probably pretty soon," Ruby yawned.

Jimmie yawned, too.

"Ruby, how old do you have to be to get a baby?"

"All depends."

"On what?" I asked.

"Your monthly time. You can't get a baby till you start bleeding...you know...
down there."

"Ruby?"

"Aren't you sleepy yet, Annie?"

"I just want to know...does it hurt the boy, too?"

"No. Boys like it," Ruby said. "They always want it. That's all that matters to
them. Mary T says a good wife lets her husband pleasure himself on her
whenever he wants. And in return she gets a baby."

"So that's why everybody gets married?" I asked.

"I guess so."

"Can we go to sleep now?" Jimmie yawned.

"All right. Goodnight."

"I'm never getting married," I whispered, and rolled over to go to sleep.

I walked Will to the front door.

"May I call you Nan?"

I about fainted when he asked me that.

May I? No one ever says that in my family. And calling me Nan is so dear. I
couldn't speak. I just nodded my head.

"Thank you again for dinner, Mrs. Sistrunk!" Will called back to the kitchen.

Mama pushed the swinging door open.

"You come back anytime, William Clock," she said, fixing her dark piercing
eyes on me.

"Yes, ma'am. Thank you," he said.

Mama went back in the kitchen and Will kissed me real quick on the
cheek and went out the door.

I nearly fainted.

Lately, I feel like fainting over every single thing, nearly every single day.

Just this morning, Mama slapped me hard and said, "Snap out of it," and
that I was no different, having my monthly just like all the other
females in the house.

But that isn't true. Mine builds up a full week before and then flows a full
week and it's awful there's so much blood.

I went back in the kitchen and sat down. My innards ached, especially
between my legs.

"Don't just sit there, Annie. Who crowned you queen?" Mama said. "Get
up and help with the dishes."

As soon as I got up from the table I knew I had to get to the washhouse
fast. It was coming on strong, but before I got to the back door, I
overflowed. Blood dripped all over the kitchen floor. I couldn't help it.

Thank goodness Will Clock isn't here to see this. I nearly fainted right
then at the thought of it.

"Oh Annie, that is disgusting!" Ruby yelled. She was married now and
thought she was so smart about everything. Her husband works the
swing-shift, so she comes to the house every day. And there she
sat, staring at me.

Everybody else at the table just looked at me, too.

Papa immediately left to go back to work. He winked at me as he hurried
out the back door. He never was one to deal with female problems.

Practically the whole blessed bunch of them was there to witness this,
except for Willie Blanton, who had been gone from home awhile.

She married right after we up and moved to California.

Mary T is gone, too. She got married last year and is over in Riverside
raising exotic birds with her no-good husband who beats her, but
Mama won't hear of it. She says Mary T made her bed and now she
has just got to sleep in it.

Jimmie just sat there as quiet as all get out. She's short like me, but real skinny and not real pretty. She never does say much. I don't think she's ever been slapped or whipped by Mama.

But Jonnie, now she had a mouth on her, even at ten-years-old. But Mama just thinks she is cute as a button. Jonnie just sat there, too, along with the two boys and little Frankie.

"Annie Beatrice," Mama cried. "When are you ever going to learn proper hygiene?"

"What's wrong with Annie?" Frankie asked.

"She's dying," Detmer joked.

"Yeah, Annie's dying," Everly chimed in, always copying everything his older brother does or says.

"Shut up!" I screamed.

"Hush all of you!" Mama snapped.

I rushed outside.

"You clean this up when you come back!" Mama called after me.

So much blood, so much blood, so much blood…and cramping. And then clots that drop out of me big as dumplings. Where does all this come from? I can't control it. I dread every month, and every month…here it comes. It's nothing like my sisters, and Mama never does talk about her own time, so there you have it. Nothing I can do but wait it out and make a mess no matter how hard I try not to.

13

Mrs. Clock, my mother-in-law, sat with perfect posture on the sofa and
sipped her coffee. Her daughter, Thelma, sat next to her, slouched
against the back of the sofa with a fox stole draped over one
shoulder, her legs crossed, exposing her knees. One free foot
swung back and forth as she stared at me.

"More coffee?" I asked.

"I don't think so," Thelma huffed.

"It's very good coffee, Nan," Mrs. Clock said.

All I could think was, I learned to make coffee when I was ten and now
here I am six years later serving it on fine china in my own home to
a fine person like Mrs. Clock.

I had to pinch myself sometimes to make sure it wasn't all a dream.

"So how's The Tribe?" Thelma asked.

"Thelma, be polite," Mrs. Clock reprimanded.

"I was just asking how her big ol' family is doing."

My face got hot. I wanted to slap her but I also wanted to make a good
impression on Will's mother. "They're fine."

"And how many of you are there again?" she asked. "I just can't keep track."

"Nine," I said. "My mother had eleven all told but two died early on. So
there's the nine of us."

Thelma looked at Mrs. Clock.

"Amazing, isn't it, Mother?"

Mrs. Clock set her cup and saucer on the end table beside her. "It must have been great fun, Nan, to grow up with so many brothers and sisters."

"Yes, ma'am," I mumbled.

If you only knew, I thought to myself. If only I could have been your child sitting there with only one brother and one sister, never beaten or spanked, spoiled rotten, wealthy, educated, tall, and beautiful.

"I certainly hope you and my brother don't plan on having a brood," Thelma sniped.

"Thelma, where are your manners?"

"Mother, no one has big families anymore. It's disgusting."

We all heard the baby in the bedroom start fussing as he woke from his nap. Thelma jumped up. "I'll get little Billy."

She went out of the room and Mrs. Clock leaned over and patted my knee. "Don't pay her any mind, Nan. She's just jealous because she doesn't have a baby of her own."

Thelma came back in carrying my baby and cooing at him.

"Are you sure you'll be alright taking care of him?" I asked.

"Don't be silly. He's my special boy," Thelma said. "He's my nephew."

Mrs. Clock gave her a sharp look. "Bring my grandson over here, Thelma."

She did as told and Mrs. Clock took him into her arms.

"He certainly is a big boy," she said.

"Takes after the Clocks," I said proudly.

"Yes, he does."

Thelma sat down beside her and the two of them focused all their attention on the baby.

"Me and Will thank you kindly for keeping Billy. We have been looking forward to the dance tonight for so long."

"You do love to dance, don't you?" asked Mrs. Clock.

"Yes, ma'am."

"Well, it is your first wedding anniversary so I don't see why a young couple shouldn't go out and celebrate."

"Yes, ma'am."

"It's not like you go out that often anyway, is it?"

"No, ma'am. But me and Will dance right here in this living room all the time." I couldn't help but smile.

"That's crazy," said Thelma.

"That's lovely, Nan," Mrs. Clock said. "And you look lovely tonight, dear. Did you get a new hair-do?"

"Thank you. It's called a marcel I got this afternoon."

"It suits you."

Thelma flung her thick, long auburn hair away from her shoulders in a huff.

"Thank you, Mrs. Clock. It comes out good seeing as how my hair is thick and curly anyway."

"Dear, I do wish you would call me Kittie."

"Oh, ma'am. I just couldn't."

Mrs. Clock smiled. "Maybe one day you will when you get more used to us."

"Yes, ma'am."

"And is that a new dress?"

"Yes, ma'am. Will bought it for me!"

"Styles certainly have changed."

"Oh Mother," Thelma piped in, "this is the Twenties. Women are free now."

Mrs. Clock glanced at the black stockings covering Thelma's legs and the dress that barely came to her knees.

"Apparently so," she sighed.

Thelma fixed her eyes on me.

"Tell me again how old my nephew is now?"

"Six months," I said, staring right back at her.

"And this is your one-year anniversary."

Go ahead. Say it, Thelma. It was a shotgun wedding. I don't care. I've got Will and that's all that matters. And I've had his baby. So there. Besides, my mother calls y'all a bunch of stuck-up Yankees. But I kept quiet and simply nodded.

"Well, well," Thelma continued. "I guess that's how tribal folk do it."

Mrs. Clock stood up. "That's enough, Thelma. Let's go. Nan, don't worry about a thing. Billy is in good hands."

"Yes, ma'am."

I helped them gather up bottles and diapers and toys and clothes, ushering all three out the door.

"Give Will our love!" Mrs. Clock called as I shut the door behind them.

I danced around the room. Free, free, free. For two whole nights I am free. Just Will and me.

I stopped in front of the mirror in the entry hall to admire the portrait staring back at me.

I loved my dress with the wide sailor collar, the V-line neck, and cap sleeves so fresh and smart—it came right to the middle of my knees. It was tailored so well—I didn't look fat. Even Jimmie couldn't sew up a dress this nice. And my Mary Jane high heels made me look so much taller; I almost came to Will's shoulder. I lifted my left hand to my shoulder and admired my gold wedding band. It looked so beautiful. I felt so lucky to be Will's wife.

The back door slammed.

"Nan, I'm home!"

"I'm in here, Honey!"

Will came into the living room.

"How do I look?" I twirled in front of him.

"Like the bee's knees."

We rushed into each other's arms.

"You're sweet as a Baby Ruth. I could eat you up," he said.

"I love you, Will. I love you."

"Happy Anniversary, Nan."

"Happy Anniversary, Darling."

I stood on my tiptoes and we kissed and kissed some more.

"Did Mother pick up Billy?"

"Yes, they just left and we're all alone. Just you and me."

"Hmmm, maybe we should stay in tonight. I can think of some things we could do."

I blushed all over.

"No, Will. I want to go dancing. You promised."

Will laughed. "Yes I did. So let me clean up and we'll be off."

I followed him into the bedroom. "I want to dance the Charleston and the Foxtrot and the Tango and the Waltz," I said.

"Is that all?"

"Oh, and the Lindy Hop."

Will took off his shirt. "We aren't going anywhere if I don't get some hot water to wash with."

"I'm sorry," I said. "I'll heat some up right away."

I hurried to the kitchen, lit the gas burner on the stove, and put on a pot of water.

My own pot. My own stove. My own kitchen. My own house. My own baby. And my very own handsome husband. No one can take that from me.

The water started to simmer so I turned off the burner and took the water into the bathroom.

"Here, Honey."

I sat on the edge of the bed while Will washed up in the bathroom.

"Was Mother alright?" he asked.

"She's fine."

"Did Thelma bring her?"

"Yes." I made a face, but his back was to me, so he didn't see it.

"It's awfully nice of them to take Billy for two days."

"It sure is," I said. "Wish they would keep him for two weeks."

"What's that you said?" he asked, lifting his face from the basin.

"Oh, nothing."

"Seems sort of empty here with him gone." He wiped his face with a towel.

"Peace and quiet," I mumbled.

Will came out of the bathroom and I stood up and hugged him.

"You smell good," I said.

We kissed. And kissed again.

"If I don't get a clean white shirt on in the next two minutes we will never leave this bedroom"

"Will!" I cried, blushing again. "It cost good money to get this hairdo. I don't want to mess it up."

"I won't mess it up. You'll see."

"But I want to go dancing."

"We'll go, don't worry. Now turn around."

I did as he said. Will unzipped my dress and I stepped out of it. He slipped it on the hanger and then picked me up in his arms and carried me to the bed. He undid the button straps on my shoes and removed them.

I admired his tall, strong body as he took off his trousers and laid them on the chair. Then he joined me in bed and finished undressing me slowly in time to the tick of the clock.

And then he made me forget about my hair, about dancing, about his bratty sister, about my tribe of a family, and even about baby Billy.

There was only me and him and me and him and me and him, and we went on that way, steady as the clock, for hours.

14

I stood on the chair while my sister Jimmie circled around me. She held
several straight pins between her lips as she pinned up the hem of
the dress she had made for me.

I can't wear any of my older sisters' hand-me-downs because I'm fatter
than all of them—especially since I had another baby.

"It's hard to believe you and Will have been married four years already,"
Jimmie said.

"I know," I sighed.

"You don't sound happy."

"I'm happy. I just wish I wasn't so heavy right now."

Well, Nan, you're still weaning the baby. Kitty's how old?"

"Eighteen months."

"See there. By the time she's two, you'll be thinning down."

I knew she was lying but I wanted to believe her just the same. I thought
back to me and Will and our first anniversary. That was the night I
conceived. The last thing I wanted was another child. All I wanted
was to go dancing. But as Jimmie teased, like the women kin in our
family I could get pregnant just ironing Will's shirts.

"Are the children still out in the yard with Mama?" I asked.

"I suppose so."

"I don't want them out there with her any longer."

"Nan, what in heaven's name is wrong with you?"

"You know how she can be."

"They're fine, I'm sure."

"She'll turn the boy against me if she can."

"Oh Nan, how can you say such things?"

"Just bring them in, would you?" There was no way I could get down without stabbing myself.

Jimmie took the pins from her mouth and stuck them into the pincushion. "Don't move," she said. "I'll be right back."

A few moments later the back door slammed.

"Mommy! Mommy!" Billy cried. "Look what Granny gave me." He opened his hand and showed me a bright copper penny.

Mama came in behind him, followed by Jimmie who was holding Kitty by the hand. Kitty was crying, as usual.

"Go put it in your piggy bank, Billy," I said, and my son ran to his room.

"What's wrong with Kitty?" I asked.

"She threw a fit because I gave a penny to the boy," Mama said. "So I paddled her bottom. That'll give her something to cry about."

Jimmie let go of Kitty's hand and came back to pinning up my hem.

Kitty waddled over to the chair I was standing on, and began screaming as loud as she could.

"Stop that, Kitty. Right now," I scolded.

She cried even louder and pounded her hands on the seat of the chair next to my feet.

"Jimmie, push her away from there."

"I can't. I've got my hands full of pins."

"Mama, pick her up or something. I can't stand her screaming!"

"Mommy! Mommy!" Billy came running in. "Can I go live with Granny? She said she'd give me a penny every week if I'm good."

I glared at Mama. "We'll see, Billy."

He ran back to his room.

Mama whisked the screaming Kitty up into her arms.

"Maybe she's hungry," I said.

"Annie, if she eats any more, she'll be fat like you when she grows up."

I ignored her. She was never going to call me Nan like Will and the others.

"Maybe she needs changing," I said.

"The child should be potty-trained by now," Mama said.

"Okay, I'm done, Nan," Jimmie said. "You can get off the chair."

Kitty quieted down to a whimper.

"Let me get out of this dress and I'll take her."

"She's alright. Leave her be," Mama said. "You know, Annie, I don't
understand you young people today. Spending good money for one
night's indulgence."

"It's our anniversary, Mama. Me and Will haven't gone out since before
Kitty was born."

"So? I had eleven children and never went out."

"Things are different now, Mama," Jimmie said softly.

"Yes, they are. And not for the better. Mark my words, Annie Beatrice. You
are in for a rude awakening if you think you can go on living this way."

"So how do you like the dress, Nan?" Jimmie asked, trying to change
the subject.

I looked at my sister's creation, but could not help but feel disappointed..
Jimmie could sew anything from a full-length strapless formal to
a three-piece double-breasted suit. I could not understand why
she put me in such a dumpy dress. Even the color—a drab green—
reminded me of a uniform.

"Thanks, Jimmie. It fits me good," I said, not wanting to hurt her feelings.

"At least it falls below those fat knees of yours," said Mama. She didn't
care whose feelings she hurt. "You're a married woman," she huffed,
"with two children. You need to dress more appropriate."

"Yes, Mama," I mumbled, but I could not look her in the eye, afraid she
would know what I was really thinking. Yes, I'm a married woman. I
ran off with Will to get away from you. But I'm only nineteen. I didn't
want two kids. I didn't even want one. But at least I gave Will a son,
so he should be satisfied. One thing's for sure, I'm not having a
brood like you did.

"When is Will getting home?" Jimmie asked, looking at the clock.

"He should be here by six. He'll clean up quick and off we go."

"Dancing, I suppose," Mama scoffed.

"Dancing and supper and more dancing," I said. This time I stared right at her.

"That leaves plenty of time for me to do up the hem," Jimmie said.

"This child weighs a ton," Mama said and set Kitty down on the floor. "Annie, you better get out of that dress if Jimmie's going to finish it in time. I'll pack a bag with the children's things."

I looked at Jimmie. "Thanks for taking them tonight."

"No need to thank me," Mama cried, thinking I was talking to her. "It's what families do."

Mama went into the kids' room. I took off the dress and put on my robe while Jimmie threaded her needle.

"Where's Kitty?"

"I don't know," Jimmie said.

"Kitty!"

A sick feeling came over me. "Kitty! Kitty, where are you?"

All of a sudden Kitty screamed.

"She's under the chair!" I cried.

"I think she's got a pin!" yelled Jimmie.

"Oh no, Kitty! Drop it. Drop it, child!"

"It's stuck in her hand," Jimmie said as she crawled under the chair to get her.

Kitty was screaming at the top of her lungs as Jimmie pulled her out.

"What happened?" Mama called.

Billy came out of the room behind her. "What's wrong?"

"She found a couple pins under the chair," Jimmie said. "I must have dropped them and didn't know it."

"Kitty, let me see," I said. "Hold still!"

It took both of us to hold her. "There's one in her mouth!"

"Oh, my God!"

"Mommy, did Kitty eat a pin?" Billy asked.

"It's all my fault!" Jimmie cried.

"No it's not. I should have been watching her!" I yelled.

We could barely hear each other for the screaming.

"You're to fault, alright," Mama said. "You're more interested in your new
    dress and going out dancing than this baby of yours. I told you no
    good would come of it."
I felt like screaming too. There goes our night out! There goes our time
    alone! There goes dancing! And having fun! Eighteen months of hell
    since that girl came into the world!
"Both of you hold her tight. I'm going to yank out those pins," Mama said.
We held Kitty as best we could as Mama pulled the pin out of the
    screaming child's hand.
""Let me see! Let me see!" yelled Billy, fascinated at the blood drops
    forming on his sister's hand.
"Now hold her good. I'll get the one out of her mouth."
It took some doing, but Mama got the last one out and then forced the
    pins into the pincushion. She did not hide her annoyance as she put
    the pincushion up on the buffet where neither child could reach it.
"Get some alcohol, Annie," Mama demanded.
I gladly let go of the screaming girl and went into the kitchen.
Will came through the back door just then, more than an hour before he
    was expected home.
"Honey, what are you doing home so early?" I asked. I hated him seeing
    me in my robe.
"What happened, Nan? I can hear the baby screaming a block away?" He
    rushed into the living room and I ran behind him.
"Baby, baby," Will said. He took Kitty from Mama and rocked her back and
    forth in his arms. "Daddy's here now. It's going to be alright, Kitty.
    Shhh, shhh. It's alright."
Kitty got quiet right away.
"Daddy! Daddy!" Billy cried.
"Hey, Buddy."
Billy threw his arms around Will's leg.
"Hello, Miss Rhoda. Hi, Jimmie. What happened, Nan?"
Me and Mama stared at each other.
"The baby found some pins," Jimmie said. "I was taking up the hem in the

dress I made for Nan and I guess I dropped a couple and didn't know it. I feel just terrible, Will."

"Jimmie, they might have fallen out when I got down off the chair," I said.

"Nobody's to blame. Accidents happen," Will said cheerfully.

"Here's some alcohol to rub on her," I said. "I'm surprised you're home so soon."

"I traded with another guy so I could have the rest of the day off. That way we could spend more time together on our anniversary."

"How sweet," Jimmie said. "Isn't that sweet, Mama?"

Mama plopped herself down on the sofa without a word.

"But now that this has happened, I think we better postpone our night out," said Will.

"What?" I asked. "You don't mean that?"

"Nan, we can't leave our child after she's been through this ordeal."

"We aren't leaving her. Mama and Jimmie are keeping the kids overnight."

"I can't let them do that," Will said. "What if Kitty got an infection or high fever or something else went wrong?"

"But Will…" I started to protest.

"We'll stay in tonight and keep our eye on her." That child had him wrapped around her little finger.

I glanced at Mama. She stared back with an I-told-you-so look.

I looked at Jimmie who stared at the floor.

"Since we won't be going out, I'm going back to work," Will said. "The guys need all the help they can get replacing that derrick that burned."

"Do you have to, Will?" I could not believe what I was hearing.

"You know I do. I'm the rig builder they hired to do the job."

"Let me fix you something to eat."

"I already ate the lunch you packed for me."

"I sure wish you didn't have to go back."

"I'll tell you what. I'll stop by Swenson's Market on the way home and get us a big steak for a late supper tonight. How's that sound?"

"If you say so," I shrugged. I had already made a pot of beans and was not looking forward to cooking again on my own anniversary.

Will laughed. "It's not the end of the world, Nan."

Kitty had fallen asleep in Will's arms. He handed her to me and kissed
        me on the forehead. Then he hugged Billy.

"Be good, Buddy. So long, everybody!"

The back door slammed behind him.

"Well then," Mama said. "I'll unpack the children's bag."

She left the room with Billy trailing right behind her.

"Oh, Nan," Jimmie said. "I feel for you. I know how disappointed you are."

I could feel tears coming on. I shoved the baby into her arms and ran
        into the kitchen to pull myself together. But as soon as I saw Will's
        dinner pail on the counter I burst out crying.

Jimmie came in holding Kitty and I dried my eyes.

"Would you mind holding her awhile?" I asked.

"Not at all, Nan."

Jimmie sat down at the table with the baby on her lap.

"See if she'll take this bottle."

Mama came into the kitchen with Billy still following her like an eager puppy.

"Kitty's probably starving after what she's been through," said Mama.

"I've got a pot of beans on the stove," I said. "The cornbread's in the oven."

Mama set the table.

"Billy, you sit here next to Aunt Jimmie."

"I want to sit next to you, Granny!"

"Granny will be on the other side of you. Sit and drink some milk."

He climbed up on the chair and began playing with his knife and spoon.

"Leave it be," I snapped. "Now drink."

Billy finished the glass of milk in a few big swallows.

"Good boy," Jimmie said. "You didn't spill a drop."

"I want some more!" he cried.

"You can wait till we eat."

"Granny! I want more milk!"

"Annie, let him have more milk. After all, he's a growing boy."

She poured him more milk as Kitty sucked away on her bottle. Maybe I
        can get her weaned, I thought.

I dished up bowls of beans for everybody.

"I want the bone, Mommy!" Billy yelled.

"Keep your voice down, Billy." I dished up the ham hock into his bowl and put it in front of him.

"What do you say?" I asked.

"Thank you."

"That's a good boy," Mama said.

We helped ourselves to the cornbread. I smeared butter on mine while it was still hot enough to melt the butter.

"There's your problem right there, Annie Beatrice," Mama said. "All that butter just turns to fat on your body. Mark my words. Not to mention it's so costly."

"Billy, take my hand," Mama said.

We all held hands and bowed our heads.

"Let us pray," Mama said. "Heavenly Father, thank you for all your blessings this year. And today we thank you for letting us come together as a family. We thank you for this food. May it nourish our bodies and souls. In Jesus Christ's name, we pray. Amen."

Billy started right away on the ham bone.

Mama, as usual, hummed a hymn as she ate. The words swam through my mind as I chewed my cornbread.

I come to the garden alone
While the dew is still on the roses
And the voice I hear falling on my ear
The Son of God discloses.

And He walks with me, and He talks with me,
And He tells me I am His own;
And the joy we share as we tarry there,
None other has ever known.

He speaks, and the sound of His voice,
Is so sweet the birds hush their singing,
And the melody that He gave to me
Within my heart is ringing.

The warm butter oozed into my mouth. "This tastes so good," I said to myself.

Mama gave me one of her disapproving looks.

After almost an hour sitting but not talking, Mama still humming, Jimmie
    said, "I think Kitty needs her diaper changed."

I sighed.

"I'll do it, Nan."

Jimmie left with the baby. Billy started banging his spoon on the table like
    it was a drum.

Mama's humming got louder.

And He walks with me, and He talks with me,
And He tells me I am His own;
And the joy we share as we tarry there,
None other has ever known.

I'd stay in the garden with Him
Though the night around me be falling,
But He bids me go; through the voice of woe
His voice to me is calling.

And He walks with me, and He talks with me,
And He tells me I am His own;
And the joy we share as we tarry there,
None other has ever known.

"My head's going to explode if you don't stop that racket, Billy."

Jimmie appeared in the doorway.

"You look like you've seen a ghost," I said.

"Nan, there's somebody at the door."

"I didn't hear the doorbell," Mama said.

"How could you with Billy banging on the table? Who is it?" I got up from
    the table. "Where's Kitty?"

"She's in her crib," Jimmie said. "Mama, you better stay in the kitchen with Billy."

A terrified feeling came over me. I don't want to go in there. I don't want to
    go to the door. Please, God.

Jimmie took my arm and led me into the living room. Two policeman stood just inside the door. I pulled back.

"Come on, Nan," Jimmie whispered.

Both men took off their hats. I started shaking my head.

No. Please, no. Don't say anything, Please, God.

"Are you Mrs. Clock?" one of them asked.

All I could do was nod my head.

"Mrs. William W. Clock?" the other officer asked.

I couldn't speak. I grabbed Jimmie's arm and held on tightly.

"There's been an accident, ma'am."

"My husband?"

They both nodded.

"Is he alright? Where is he? What happened? Can I see him? Where is he?"

Jimmie held me close to her.

"He was killed," one said.

"No!" I screamed.

"He stepped back and missed the scaffolding. His fellow workers saw it happen," the other officer said.

"No! Dear God, no!"

"He fell a hundred and twenty feet."

"I don't understand!"

"Ma'am, that's like falling off the top of a twelve-story building."

My knees started trembling.

"They rushed him to the hospital," the officer continued, "but he was already dead. We're awful sorry, Mrs. Clock."

The policemen left.

"No! Oh, my beloved Will! My life. My whole life. Oh, Will, my God. If only he hadn't gone back to work! If it hadn't been for Kitty he would be here now."

"Nan, don't talk like that."

Mama and Billy came into the living room.

"What is it?" Mama asked.

"My Will is dead! I don't want to live without him!" I screamed. "I might as well be dead, too!"

"Mommy!" Billy cried.

I looked at him, dazed. He has the Sistrunk's dark hair and eyes, but he's a big boy, like his daddy. And now he's all I have left of Will.

Kitty started crying from her crib in the bedroom.

"Let her cry, for all I care! I don't want anything to do with that child!"

"Annie Beatrice, don't say such things," Mama scolded.

"Will would be alive right now if it wasn't for her!" I screamed.

"Oh, Nan. You don't mean it," Jimmie said.

"Yes I do."

"I'll see to the baby." Jimmie said and left the room.

I pulled Billy to me.

"Our son. Our one and only son," I cried. "Daddy's never coming home again. Never ever."

Billy started crying.

"You come with Granny," Mama said to him. "We'll go out in the yard and you can swing on the tire."

I looked around the living room.

This is the room where Will and I danced and laughed and held each other. The room where we lived. And now he's dead. We'll never dance again. It feels so empty now. It's not a living room anymore. It's a dying room. I wish I could die in it right now. I wish I could climb to the top of that derrick. I would jump off and join you, my darling, my dearest. Oh, the thought of you dying like that! I can't stand it!

"My life is over," I sobbed. "I'll never be happy again."

Kitty

15

I never take good pictures.
Whenever I smile I look terrible.
And when I don't smile I look mean.
It's my mouth.

One time my brother beat me up so bad he dislocated my jaw. My mouth
   was never the same after that. As usual, my mother just watched. I
   think she encouraged him sometimes.
She, herself, never lifted a hand against me, and she never raised her
   voice either, but she sure let Bill beat the living hell out of me.
And that's how I went blind.
Another time he beat me around my face so hard he closed one of my
   eyes. I was blind in that eye for a long time. I was never able to see
   out of it real well after that. Then I had to start wearing glasses.
   Eventually I lost my sight all together.
The beatings always happened when Ira was at work. Mother made
   sure of that.
I ran around a lot. I guess that's why she let Bill beat me. But that only
   made me crazier, and made me want to stay away from the house
   even more. I'd stay out real late; sometimes I might not come home
   for a day or two. Then I'd pay the price. It became the routine.

It's not like we were kids. We were both teenagers. Bill was two years older than me. And big. And really strong.

He took after Mother's dad, William Sistrunk, that way. William Sistrunk was my grandfather. He died when I was eight.

My grandmother wasn't a big woman. Her name was Rhoda Florence but we called her Grandma Sisser. I think I got my small bone structure from her. Two of Mother's sisters, Jimmie and Jonnie True, were real tiny.

Mother was small, too. But she carried a lot of weight. No one else in the family was heavy like her. She was almost as wide as she was tall. I never saw her in anything but a house dress or a muu-muu.

The day of that particular beating Gordon was on furlough and I was filling my days with him. We kissed for the longest time. It was luscious. He drove off and I ran inside to my room. I always cried when one of my fellas left. All of a sudden, my bedroom door flew open. Mother stood there. "You are no good," she screamed.

I sneered at her. I was so tired of being told how bad I was.

"Just because men like me?" I replied.

"Bill, come in here and teach your sister a lesson!" Mother called.

My brother charged into the room more than eager to let me have it.

"You are a tramp," Mother said. "When I was your age I was married and already had one child."

"So?" I screamed back. "That makes you a saint? You probably had to get married!"

Mother stepped back like I had slapped her.

"You will pay for this, Kitty Annabelle Clock," she said calmly, and nodded her head at Bill.

My brother hauled off and slugged me in the face. I fell to the floor howling with pain. Mother left the room and Bill kicked me once in the stomach. I doubled up before he could kick me again.

"Maybe that'll teach you not to upset Mama," he said. "I'm ashamed to live in the same house as you. I sure wouldn't marry no girl who's gone with as many guys as you have."

"No girl would marry you anyway," I mumbled as blood filled my mouth.

He started to swing at me with his open hand but I stuck both my arms up over my head and blocked him.

"Why don't you just leave and never come back?" he snarled.

"Maybe I will," I said.

Bill stomped out of the room. I could barely see him. One of my eyes had already closed shut.

Our step-dad, Ira, came home early from work right about then. Bill stormed out of the room as Ira came into the house. Ira headed directly to my room.

"What is going on here?" he demanded.

Mother just stood there. "Nothing," she said. "Nothing is going on." Her wide, four foot, ten-inch tall frame filled the doorway.

We all heard the kitchen door slam as Bill took off. Big, brave Bill...afraid of Dad, I thought. I called him Dad because he was the only father I had ever known. Our real father, William Clock, died when I was only eighteen months old. He fell off an oil derrick that he was repairing after a fire. Mother married him when she was barely fifteen and he was twenty-one. I'm still convinced that she had to get married.

They had only four years together when the accident happened. The newspaper article that Mother saved all those years claimed he fell one hundred twenty feet—that's the same as falling off a twelve-story building. His death left her with two kids and no way to support herself. Everyone assumed her marriage to him was a way up and out. Her dreams of a long and prosperous life full of love vanished in a moment.

Dad looked at me. "Kitten, are you going to tell me what happened?"

I blurted out. "Bill beat me up. And it's not the first time either."

The shock was apparent on his face. He just couldn't believe it.

Mother glared at me.

"Nan, is that true?"

"Kitty is lying," Mother said.

"I am not!" I yelled.

For a minute I thought he was actually going to slug her. I had never seen him so angry. But he had never raised his hand to her or to me or Bill. Maybe because we weren't really his kids. He and Mother had no children of their own.

Ira was a bachelor. He raised his younger brothers after their mother ran off and left them and their father. I'm not sure how Mother and Ira met. But they eventually settled into a modest tract house in Anaheim that backed up to the freeway. Dad worked as a tool-and-die man.

Their actual arrangement as husband and wife was confusing to me. The whole time I lived at home they had separate bedrooms. Mother kept dolls and stuffed animals on her bed. Dad kept his loaded pistol under a pillow on his. I never saw them hug or kiss or even touch each other except on the rare occasion when Dad took her by the arm and helped her in and out of the car.

"If..." Ira said tensely, "...if this ever happens again...if Bill ever lays so much as a finger on Kitty again... I will leave this house and not come back. I swear, Annie."

Mother knew he was serious. He never used her real name, no one did. Everyone called her Nan. She hated the name Annie.

I was still trembling when Dad walked out of the room.

Mother had no choice; he was the breadwinner. She didn't work, other than cooking and cleaning. She had been a housewife all her life. Not because she loved it or wanted to stay home with us kids or anything like that. I think she stopped caring when my real dad was killed. He was the love of her life. Aunt Jimmie told me they used to go dancing all the time. And Mother would play the piano for him and anyone else who happened by to visit.

But after he was killed, Mother gave all that up.

Mother became a dumpy housewife, which was very different than her sisters. Aunt Jimmie and Aunt Frankie were both artists; they painted all the time. Aunt Jonnie, who we called Tootsie, was real creative, too. But she was restless. Even their older sister, Mary T, had a passion raising and selling exotic birds.

But my mother gave up when my real father died. She never even learned to drive. She refused to go anywhere; Ira even had to do the grocery shopping. I couldn't stand the thought of what would become of us if he left. I knew he would stay, if only for me.

"I hope you're happy now," Mother hissed, and slammed the door behind her.

16

I loved every boy I went out with. Unfortunately, every one of them went
  overseas; some never came back, which made me sad. But I was
  glad to spend time with each and every one of them. We laughed
  and danced and danced and danced.

So what if I went to bed with them. It wasn't my fault boys liked me. I had
  a really good figure. Besides, every single one of them was good to
  me and treated me real sweet.

Bill Kenaga, from Kansas, was my true love.

Then there was Don Douglas, Andy Sittliffe, and Otto Hora.

Sammy Tillery, Alvie Blessing, Bob Wright, and Glenn.

George L, Dick Preciado, Jimmy Megelene, and Wayne.

Stan Freed, Chuck Graham, and Delbert O. Van Liew (we called him Buddy).

Dickie Brown, Bob Bookout, Morgan Wiley, and Roi from Riverside.

Lane Excelsior, Jerry Raul, and Oz.

Frank and Scotty, George and Bob, and Fred.

Gordon Darrell Baker and Elmer.

I remember them all.

What did Mother know? She'd been with only two men in her life. My
  real father, William Clock, and Ira Wolcott, my stepfather, who I'm
  convinced she never had sex with.

I know she had sex at least twice in her life because my brother and I were living proof. But beyond that, it's anyone's guess. I figured Aunt Jimmie knew, but I never asked her.

In my mother's day, and even when I was a girl, most girls got married before they would ever let the guy touch them. But it was too late for me to walk down the aisle in a white gown. Thanks to the neighbor man.

He raped me when I was fourteen.

After that I went and lived with Aunt Jimmie. I don't remember if I went to get away from Mother or if Mother sent me away. It didn't matter. I was free—free and having a ball—with boys.

I finished high school in Riverside and danced every night of the week if I wanted to. Aunt Jimmie never got upset and never once told on me.

I was the first one in our family to get a high school diploma. Mother never got one and her mother, Grandma Sisser, never even went to high school. Marriage and babies was all she knew. And her mother before that. And her mother before that.

Me and a bunch of girls liked to pile in somebody's car and go to the beach whenever we could . My closest friends were always there for me. Especially Joyce Lee Conner, Jeanne Walker, and Judy Lovejoy who I met the week I went to live with Aunt Jimmie. Then there was Bettye Lou Jones and my cousin Edwana, who we called Eddie.

Edwana was Aunt Tootsie's daughter, but Tootsie was always running around. When she had her baby, she left Eddie with Aunt Jimmie. Seemed like Tootsie was always leaving town with one man or another. Eddie never knew her father, but Tootsie came back to visit her from time to time and brought her tons of presents and expensive gifts, which thrilled Eddie. But Tootsie could only stand a couple days or so in Riverside. She'd get antsy after awhile and find some reason to leave again. I kinda knew how Eddie felt, not having a real dad, so I let her tag along after me. She was like my little sister. We always had fun.

One day, Jeanne came flying into the jewelry store where I worked. "Kitty, guess what?"

Lucky for her, I was there alone. Mr. Glass, the owner, had to run an errand and he trusted me to mind the store while he was gone. His daughter Kay and I were in the same class in high school. She got married right after we graduated and followed her husband when he got shipped overseas.

I loved my job. I got to stay with Aunt Jimmie, so I didn't have to pay room and board. I bought the most expensive underwear I could afford. By the time I was eighteen, I owned twenty-four pairs of shoes. I danced so much I needed that many. I never felt guilty. I only spent what I earned.

"What's going on?" I asked.

"My brother is in town on leave."

"Sooooo....?" I said.

"So, you know. I want you to meet him," Jeanne said. " You know I've been talking about him for as long as you and I've been running around together. So now he's here. You've just gotta meet him," she insisted.

"Are you talking about Bruce or Tom?"

"Tom is my younger brother."

"I don't mind 'em young," I teased.

Jeanne laughed. "Tommy's already hitched with a gal named Irene. So forget him. Bruce is good-looking, just your type. So what do you say?"

"Of course. You know me."

"Great! What time do you get off?"

"Five."

"Perfect. We'll meet you at the drugstore."

"Shouldn't I go home and change first?"

"No, you look fabulous as always. You know you have the best figure around. You could wear a flour sack and look fantastic. Wish I was built like you."

"Thanks, Jeanne. You're sweet."

"Instead of getting it up here, I got it all down here," she said, patting her rear end.

"Don't worry, you still got what it takes," I said.

"Thanks."

"Will George be going with us too?"

"You're darn right he will be," Jeanne said.

Jeanne and her fiancé, George Cessna, had planned to get married in August. They were crazy about each other. George had just gotten out of the service and already had himself a real good job running heavy equipment for a company that builds bridges.

"A double date. How fun," I said.

"Yep. See you later then," Jeanne said and hurried out the door.

I took out the dust cloth and walked around the store wiping fingerprints off the glass cases. I loved seeing all the sparkling jewelry. Diamonds, rubies, emeralds, sapphires, each precious gem, beautiful and clean, and perfectly formed soft, round pearls. I loved the polished platinum, silver and gold, and the elegant watches that kept perfect time.

I loved every minute I spent in the store. Each morning I got to help Mr. Glass bring the jewelry out of the safe and put it on display. At the end of the day we put every ring, bracelet, pair of earrings, gold chains, and carved silver bracelets back into the safe.

Mr. Glass let me try on the jewelry whenever we weren't busy. He'd say, "You can't sell what you don't know and love." He'd encourage me to surround myself with beautiful things. He'd say, "The more comfortable you are around these precious items, the more comfortable you will be selling them to those who have the money to buy them."

After Jeanne left, I took out a large cameo brooch and pinned it on my jacket. I liked to wear suits to work. Very nice ones, tailor-made just for me by Aunt Jimmie. She was the seamstress in the family. "As you sew, so shall you rip," she always said. I admired the pin in the mirror and then put it back in the case just as Mr. Glass walked in the door.

"That took longer than I thought," he said, taking off his hat and coat.

"Everything alright?"

"Oh, fine. Any business while I was gone?"

"Not a soul. Well, my friend Jeannie came by. But, of course, she didn't buy anything."

"You need wealthier friends, Kitty," he joked.

"Yes, sir," I laughed. "But, if you remember, I did sell her fiancé their engagement ring."

"That's true."

"And I know for a fact George will be purchasing their wedding rings from us too."

"Marriage is good business for people like us."

I really liked when Mr. Glass talked to me that way, like I was his equal... almost. I sometimes imagined myself owning a jewelry store of my own, or maybe this very one. Someday, when Mr. Glass was ready to retire.

"Not only do we get to sell weddings rings and gold bands," he said. "But marriage leads to babies who need sterling silver drinking cups and feeding spoons."

"And the little crystal I.D. bracelets," I said.

"Exactly. And don't forget, marriage also leads to anniversaries."

"Hopefully, twenty or thirty or forty of them," I said.

We both glanced around at all the various items that would be perfect anniversary gifts.

"And then there's birthdays," I said. "The wife's birthday. The husband's birthday."

"Exactly," said Mr. Glass. "A special necklace for her."

"A handsome set of cufflinks for him."

"And when their children get older..."

"...a charm bracelet for the daughter," I said, picking one up from the display case that I wished I could afford for myself.

"Or a nice watch for the boy when he turns sixteen," Mr. Glass said.

I put the bracelet back.

"Or little diamond studs for the girl when she graduates from high school," I said.

"Yes, marriage makes for good business," he said. "Speaking of which, when do you plan to get married, Kitty?"

"Me? Never!"

"Oh come now. It's every girl's dream to walk down the aisle and be a beautiful blushing bride."

"It's not my dream."

"You mean to tell me you don't have one steady fella out of all those
boyfriends of yours?"

"No, sir, I don't," I said. I tried not to blush.

"Well, you will one day."

"I hope not. I'm having too much fun. I don't want things to change," I said.
"Besides, Mr. Glass, I really like working here. I hope you know that."

"I know, Kitty. But you can't do this forever. You should settle down and have a
family of your own."

"Why?"

He paused for a moment. "Because that's the way life is. People get married.
Women stay at home and raise kids and take care of the house and
make sure their husbands are looked after. And the man works and
provides for his wife and family."

"And they all live happily ever after, I suppose."

"Hopefully," he said. "And hopefully they come in our store to buy gifts for one
another."

Not my mother. Not my family. We don't live happily ever after. Never have.
Ira doesn't buy Mother any jewelry. She would never wear it if even if he
did. And she doesn't buy him anything because she has no money of her
own. These thoughts bounced through my head as Mr. Glass boasted
about his daughter.

"Look at my Kay," said Mr. Glass. "She's already married and now she is
expecting. This will be our first grandchild."

"I'm happy for you," I said. "And for her."

"You can't have fun forever, Kitty."

"Well, I'm sure gonna try! In fact, I've got a date at five o'clock if that's alright
with you, Mr. Glass."

We both looked at the towering grandfather clock with its stern pendulum
tick-tocking back and forth declaring the time to be four-thirty.

"That's fine, Kitty, It's been quiet this afternoon. Why don't you start putting
things in the safe. I can finish up when you leave."

"Oh, thank you so much, Mr. Glass. Jeannie's brother is in town on leave and she's been wanting me to meet him for the longest time."

"Well, we can't have you miss an opportunity like that," he said with a smile.

"No, sir!"

I took the fragile pearl necklace and draped it in the palm of my left hand. With my right hand, I carried the matching earrings. Mr. Glass opened the door to the safe room and I went in, which always made me feel as if I was entering a sacred place, bringing precious offerings, like to Baby Jesus in the manger or to an ancient god.

The safe felt so…well, so safe. I carefully placed the pearls on the cushioned counter, picked up the black velvet tray, and went back out for more. I always admired how the diamonds and platinum gold and sterling silver looked so rich on the black tray. I preferred the rubies and garnets and sapphires on a backdrop of white or cream, while the opals and emeralds stood out better on a plain silver tray, as did the turquoise and onyx. To me, all of the jewelry was so perfect…unspoiled. No scratches or nicks or bloody bruises. Pure and perfect and worth everything.

I took a deep breath. The grandfather clock bonged five times loud and clear.

"I better go!" I cried, grabbing my purse.

"You better go," Mr. Glass repeated.

"See you tomorrow!'

"Have fun!" he called, locking the door behind me.

I rushed down the sidewalk to the drugstore. Jeanne and George waved me over to where they were sitting at one of the little tables.

"Hey there, Lover Girl," George said.

"Hi, Gorgeous George." I sat down with them. "Where's your brother?" I asked Jeanne.

"Right behind you," she said. "He just walked in."

I turned and saw a man in a sailor's uniform coming towards our table.

He was the classic tall, dark, and handsome type with a big grin on his face that showed off a slight little gap between his two front teeth, which made him all the more charming.

"Kitty, this is my brother, James Bruce Gaulden."

"Hello'" I smiled and extended my hand.

"Bruce, this is my dear friend Kitty Clock."

"Hello, Kitty," he said, and gently shook my hand.

"Sit down, sailor," George said.

"How you doing, Georgie Porgie?" Bruce slapped George on the back and sat down.

"Don't do that again or I'll deck you," George said.

"Uh-oh. Big Army man talking. I better look out."

"Come on, you two," said Jeannie. "Let's all try to get along and have a good time."

I looked at George and then at Bruce. Bruce winked at me and smiled. "So what's everybody drinking?" he asked.

"I've got a cherry coke," Jeannie said.

"I've got a rum and coke," said George.

"Rum? In the drugstore? Since when did they start allowing drugstores to sell liquor? Boy, things have changed since I've been gone. And that's been too long," Bruce said. He winked at me again.

"No, dummy," George replied. "I've got the rum right here." George opened one side of his jacket to reveal a flask in the inside pocket.

"Sounds good to me," I said. "I just got off work and I'm parched."

"You got enough in there for both of us?" Bruce asked.

"Sure," said George. "There's more where this came from in my truck."

Bruce went over to the counter and ordered two cokes.

"So what do you think so far?" Jeannie whispered.

"You told me he was handsome, but good grief! I nearly fell over."

Jeannie laughed. "I thought you two would hit it off."

Bruce sat down with the drinks. George added splashes of rum to both and we all made toasts.

"To life, liberty, and the pursuit of happiness!"

"Here's mud in your eye!"

"Down the hatch!"

"To freedom!"

"And the end of the war!"

"Yankee Doodle went to town," Jeannie sang.

"Anchors aweigh, my boys, anchors aweigh," sang Bruce.

"I need another drink," George said and got up.

"George, why don't you wait? We'll go eat pretty soon and we can get drinks then."

"Goddamit Jeanne, I want another drink now. Not later," he snapped.

George went over to the counter.

Jeannie shrugged. "You two want another?"

"I'm fine, honey," I said.

"I'll have another with George so he isn't drinking alone," said Bruce.

He got up and joined George at the counter.

"Don't worry, Jeannie. George is a big man. He can handle more liquor than the rest of us combined."

"I suppose you're right," she said.

"I am, honey."

"So you like Bruce?" she said, changing the subject

"I like Bruce. I really, really like Bruce."

We hugged each other as the boys returned to the table.

"What was that about?" George asked.

"Girl stuff," Jeannie said.

"Well, how about a hug for poor ol' George?"

Jeanne wrapped her arms around his big shoulders and they kissed each other so long that Bruce and I both started feeling uncomfortable watching them.

"Now, now," Bruce teased. "You'll have plenty of time for that after the wedding."

Jeanne and George both laughed.

"Maybe we should leave you two lovebirds alone," I said.

Bruce put his arm around me. "Or maybe we should take a walk around the block together."

I looked at him. Our noses nearly touched, we were so close. I could feel myself melting. He stared into my eyes and just grinned and grinned. I stared back.

"Maybe we should leave you two alone," Jeanne joked.

"Maybe you should," I mumbled.

Bruce pressed his mouth against mine and we locked in a kiss that I wanted to last forever.

"Absolutely not!" cried Jeanne. "Let's drink up and go to The Wharf. I'm starving. And I'm dying for one of their dry martinis."

"Now you're talking!" George said.

We quickly finished our drinks and headed for The Wharf in George's car.

Bruce and I sat in the back and he held my hand.

"After we eat, let's go dancing," I said.

Jeanne looked at George.

Nobody said anything.

"What's wrong? C'mon George, you and Jeanne need to practice for that first dance at your wedding."

George just shrugged.

"Well then, Bruce and I will go without you."

I felt Bruce's hand stiffen in mine. He just stared straight ahead.

"Now what? Don't tell me you don't want to dance either?"

"That's right, I don't," Bruce said.

I pulled my hand away. "I can't believe this."

Jeanne looked at me. "Maybe we can go listen to some jazz after we eat," she said.

"Is there any place around here that plays country music?" asked Bruce.

"If you want to listen to that goddam shit-kickin' music, then go back to Arkansas," said George.

"Now George, don't start in on him," Jeanne said.

"All these goddam oakies moving to California…" George grumbled.

"So you're saying I'm an oakie?" Jeanne cried.

"No, hell no. But your goddam brother sure is."

"I'll be sure to play my mandolin on your grave, George," Bruce replied.

"Oh, shut up both of you," I said. "I want to know why you won't go dancing with me, Bruce."

"I don't know how."

"Is that all? I can teach you."

"No," he said. "I can't learn. I've already tried. And I'm not getting out there in front of everybody and making a fool of myself."

"Nobody will be watching you."

"That's what you think."

"We're here," George said as we pulled up to the restaurant.

"Boy, this is some night. I can't wait to have that martini," I said.

Jeanne and I got out of the car and walked inside together.

"Don't be too hard on him, Kitty. He's just shy. He'll come around. I bet you'll have him out on the dance floor in no time."

"I hope so. I just can't imagine going through life not dancing."

17

I looked around. Boxes, boxes. Nothing but boxes.

"This is a big move for you," said my neighbor friend, Bonnie. She folded linens and placed them in one of the boxes.

"I know," I replied. "I've never lived anywhere but here in Downey. Or Riverside before I got married."

"And now Oregon of all places," Bonnie said.

"That's what the doctor ordered. You know how bad Will's asthma is. Didn't I tell you Dr. Reynolds said we had to get him out of here?"

"You did. But why Oregon?"

"He said Will needs to be in a place that has all four seasons. I picked Oregon since my Aunt Tootsie and Uncle Earl are there. Thank God it isn't all that far away."

"That's true. Better than having to move to Minnesota or New England!" We both laughed.

"I'm sure going to miss you, sweetie," Bonnie said.

"Same here, Bonnie."

"You promise to write now," she ordered.

"I will. And you better write back."

I gave my friend a big hug.

The kitchen screen door slammed. Will ran through the kitchen with Bonnie's son right behind him.

"Mark! Don't run in the house!" Bonnie cried.

"Will, come back here!" I called.

Both boys burst into the kitchen. Will wheezed and panted.

"Dammit, Will. Listen to yourself," I said. "Slow down. Otherwise I'll be up half the night with you."

"Aw, Mom," Will grumbled.

"You heard me," I said.

"But Mom, I wasn't running very fast," he argued.

"How would you like to carry your teeth in your back pocket?" I threatened.

Will made a face and stared at his feet.

"No more backtalk," I said. "Now where's your sister?"

"I guess she's in the backyard."

"I told you to keep an eye on her. You're supposed to be the big brother."

"She was playing with Chrissy."

"And where've you been?" I asked.

"Riding bikes," Will answered.

Just then Bonnie's daughter came to the door.

"Mom, I'm hungry," Chrissy said through the screen.

"Hang on," Bonnie replied. "We're going home in a minute."

"Chrissy, where's Steed?" I asked.

"I don't know."

Bonnie and I looked at each other in alarm.

"Come inside, honey," Bonnie said.

Chrissy came into the kitchen and clung to her mother.

"Now tell us where Steed is," Bonnie said.

"She went away," Chrissy said matter-of-factly.

I ran out the door.

"Steed! Steed!" I called. "Time to come home! Steed!"

She didn't answer.

Oh my God, I thought to myself. Somebody's taken her. I've told her and told her not to talk to strangers. And if anybody pulls up in a car for her to run like hell. Dammit!

I went back inside. Bonnie looked as worried as I felt.

"Will, go look for your sister. Ride your bike up Duessler and Brunache Street, too. Call her name. Ask anybody who's out in their yard if they've seen her. Go on. Go! Now!"

"Go with him, Mark," Bonnie said.

The two boys took off full of excitement. Obviously they thought it was fun being ordered to go ride their bicycles. I had no other choice. I don't have a car and neither does Bonnie. We're housewives and our husbands drive the cars back and forth to work.

"Now, Chrissy," I began, trying to calm myself. "What were you and Steed doing before she went away?"

"Playing under the tree."

"In the backyard?"

"Uh-huh."

"Did she leave you there?"

"Uh-huh."

"How long ago was this?"

"I don't know," Chrissy answered.

Of course she doesn't know, I thought. She's only four just like Steed.

"Mommy, I'm hungry."

"In a minute," Bonnie replied.

"Here, Chrissy. Have a cookie," I said. "I made them this morning. They're Steed's favorite," I said to Bonnie, fighting back tears.

The little girl started chomping away at the chocolate chip cookie.

"What do you say?" Bonnie asked.

"Thank you," Chrissy said with crumbs falling out of her mouth.

"You're welcome," I said. "Did Steed say where she was going?"

"A girl came and got her."

"What? Who?" I exclaimed.

"A girl came down the driveway and wanted us to walk to the grocery store with her," she said nonchalantly.

"Oh my God," I gasped. "To the Alpha Beta Market?"

Chrissy nodded as she finished her cookie.

I looked at Bonnie.

"That's a good mile away," I said.

"And on that busy road too," Bonnie said.

"There's no sidewalks between here and the Alpha Beta," I added.

"Honey, who was the girl?" Bonnie asked.

"I don't know."

"Why didn't you go with Steed?" I asked impatiently.

"I didn't want to. It's hot outside. Besides, I'm hungry," Chrissy said.

"Bonnie, would you find Will and take him home with you? I've got to go look for Steed."

"Of course, Kitty. Don't worry. She's probably already on her way back home."

"She better be. Steed knows better than to do anything without my permission. I'll teach her a thing or two."

Bonnie went out the screened door with Chrissy.

"Don't be too hard on her, Kitty. I'm sure she didn't realize how far the store really was."

"She'll realize it when I get through with her."

I waited till Bonnie and Chrissy walked down the driveway and disappeared around the corner. Then I took the yardstick from its hook behind the kitchen door and started walking as fast as I could towards the grocery store.

That child is going to pay for this. She could be grabbed up by anybody. Or run over by a car. What kind of mother will people think I am, letting a four-year-old go off by herself. And all she's wearing is her swimsuit. She's probably barefoot, too. I can't even control my own children. How dare Steed disobey me. Will is enough trouble. I can't take two of them being little shits. I'm about at my wit's end. All I do is cook, clean house, wash and iron, shop on a dime budget, and run after these damn kids. I don't even own a decent pair of underpants anymore.

"Oh my God, there she is," I said aloud. I was only thirty feet from the house.

Steed and an older girl were walking towards me, talking and laughing. I stopped in the street and just stood there waiting. Steed finally saw me and waved.

Who does she think she is going off like this and laughing and thinking it's all so funny? Well, she can think again.

"I'll wipe that smile off her face real fast," I said aloud.

The two walked up to me.

"Hi, Mommy," Steed said, looking a little surprised to see me.

I ignored her and stared at the girl.

"Who are you?" I demanded.

"Brenda," she replied, slowly.

"Well, Brenda. I suggest you get yourself home right now. And don't ever
come into our yard again. Do you understand me?"

The girl took off running down the street.

"What in the hell do you think you're doing?" I screamed.

"What did I do?" Steed gave me a confused look. I grabbed her upper arm.

"Don't act like you don't know!"

I yanked her around and smacked the back of her bare legs with the
yardstick. Steed screamed at the top of her lungs.

"Go ahead and scream!" I yelled. "You scared me half to death going off like
that without my permission!"

Steed fought to pull away from me but I held her tight and dragged her down
the street towards home.

"Mommy, no!"

I don't care if the neighbors see me or not. I'll be damned if I'm going to let
this child get away with anything.

Steed struggled to get loose but I just kept beating her with the yardstick
until it finally broke.

She screamed and cried and choked all at the same time.

"Never do that again!" I cried.

She pulled away from me and ran into the house.

I went slowly up the back steps into the kitchen.

My legs feel like two sacks of wet cement.

I plopped down at the kitchen table.

I feel so exhausted and drained.

I heard Steed bawling her eyes out in her bedroom. The broken yardstick lay
on the table. I lit a cigarette.

My hands are shaking. I'm shaking.

Steed's crying turned to sobs and then pathetic gasps for air.

I can't stand to hear her cry like that. It makes me feel like crying, too.

I picked up the telephone and dialed.

"Bonnie, I'm back. Yes, I found her. Everything's fine. You can send Will home now. Thanks for all your help. I'll talk to you tomorrow."

I hung up the phone.

Not a sound came from beyond the kitchen. I tiptoed to Steed's room and carefully opened the door. Steed lay face down on the bed.

"Steed?" I said softly.

I walked over to the edge of the bed. Big red welts flared up across the back of her little legs. I put my hand out to touch them and Steed suddenly turned over.

She shrieked at me in utter terror. "No, Mommy, no! Don't hurt me again!"

She scrambled off the bed.

"Please don't hurt me anymore! Please don't hurt me!" Steed cried.

I stepped back, stunned. "Honey, I'm sorry."

Steed cowered in the corner of the room like a trapped animal. I walked towards her and she started weeping and shaking all over.

"I'm sorry, honey," I said, not going any closer. "I'm really sorry. I'm not mad anymore."

She watched me, eyes wild, full of fear and distrust.

"I'll bring something to put on your legs."

I went back to the kitchen. And then it hit me hard.

I've broken far more than a yardstick. I broke something today I will never be able to repair. Not ever.

I slumped into a chair and sobbed.

Steed

18

"Mom! Help!"

Comanche took off with me hanging on.

Mom and Dad and Uncle Earl stood there by the barn getting smaller as
Comanche flew across the field with me on his back.

I could barely hear Aunt Tootsie as she ran out of the house yelling,
"Gawd dammit, Earl. Go after her!"

After that, I couldn't hear anything but the wind.

Nothing but wind in my face.

Wind in my eyes.

Wind in my ears.

Wind in my mouth as I screamed.

Faster and faster and faster we went.

Just me and the Shetland pony.

My braids were flapping against my neck like two ropes. I was barefoot. I
tried keeping my feet in the stirrups but my legs were too short. My
legs kept slapping against the pony. What made it worse was I was
wearing shorts so my legs were getting rubbed and burned.

Comanche charged past the salt lick where me and Will liked to knock
off pieces and suck on them after we played Cowboys and Indians.
Then we'd run over the top of the hill and look for the sheep. The
same flock me and the pony were headed straight for.

Suddenly, Uncle Earl came up next to us on his horse just before we hit the sheep. He threw a lasso around Comanche's neck and next thing you know we were trotting.

And then stopping.

"You alright, Peanut?"

That's what he liked to call me. Peanut.

"Yeah." I couldn't say much. I just looked at my uncle as he sat high up on his horse, holding the rope around the pony's neck as the sheep wandered off.

Uncle Earl had real black hair and real blue eyes and tattoos on his arms from when he was in the Navy. He had a big smile with real white teeth. Aunt Tootsie was always mad at him for one reason or another.

"Good girl. You rode the little bastard like a regular cowboy. I'm proud of you."

Uncle Earl led me and the pony back to the barn where Mom and Dad stood.

As soon as we got close enough, Mom screamed, "Don't ever do that again! You scared me to death!"

She pulled me off the pony and smacked my rear-end before I knew what was happening.

"Now, Kitty…" Uncle Earl started to say. But I knew nobody had better try and talk to Mom when she's mad.

"She could've been killed! Jeezus, you men don't think!" Mom yelled.

Dad took the reins without saying anything and walked Comanche into the barn.

"That's right, Bruce," Mom said. "Walk off and let me be the heavy here! You never do anything." She followed my dad into the barn.

I took off running. I had to find my big brother, Will.

All I had was Will and Dollie, my doll. I didn't have no sisters like some other kids.

We got a kitten once from Aunt Tootsie. She showed me how to tell if it was a boy or girl. It was easy. Mom said we couldn't have a girl cat because they're too much trouble and have babies and stuff. So I picked out the orange boy and named him Herman.

Mom said he had to stay outside after she found his poop inside the woodstove. She said he had diarrhea. So something was wrong with him and he had to stay outside. Poor Herman. I made a bed for him inside a cardboard box with part of an old blanket. The box sat on the back porch.

There was a roof over it so he was safe out of the rain.

It got colder and colder and pretty soon there was snow and ice. And one morning Herman didn't move. I found him dead in his box curled into a tight, hard ball of cold orange fur. I cried and Mom said it was better he was dead because he was real sick.

Dad dug a whole out in the garden and buried Herman while I stayed inside the warm house and watched through the window. He sawed up a couple pieces of wood and made a cross. Then he painted it blue because that was the only paint there was in the barn. I kept watch while Dad pounded the cross into the ground on top of Herman's grave.

One night when it was real cold I woke up and looked out my window. At first I couldn't see anything because the glass was all white with frozen snowflakes. But I kept looking because I heard somebody call my name. Grown-ups always said I made things up, but this is the God-honest truth. But no one ever listened or believed anything I said.

Anyway, I could finally see through the dark and there, glowing above the blue cross, was an angel. She had called my name. It was her voice that woke me up. As soon as I saw her golden light I felt really warm and good inside like when Aunt Tootsie would hug me and hold me real close for a long time. I just want to stay in Aunt Tootsie's arms forever. I got back under the covers feeling happy that my cat had gone to heaven. I guess I fell asleep because the next time I opened my eyes the sun was shining through the window.

I never told one single person about the angel. Not even Will.

Me and Will played outside all the time, except when it was raining. But even in the snow we'd go out and find stuff to do. That's 'cause we were the only kids for miles. Everybody lived on farms and ranches so you couldn't see another house from ours. The Murphy kids lived way down the road but Mom said it was too far for us to walk. She had to drive us if we wanted to play with them and the only time that happened was when Mom wanted to visit with Mrs. Murphy.

Every chance we got Will and me would run as fast as we could to the creek. It seemed to be miles from our house because it always took forever to get there. We'd walk and climb and look at things like the beaver dam under the pile of logs in the middle of the creek. Sometimes we'd see the beavers go in or come out of their house, swimming with their funny, flat tails. We'd have to be real quiet or they'd hide under the water in their house and never come back out.

I liked the waterfall part the best. That's what Will called it, anyway. "A waterfall." The creek had a bunch of big rocks in this one part and you could hear the water go crashing over the rocks before you even got there. It made so much noise we'd have to yell at each other.

Everywhere we went the creek made different sounds. Some places the water got pretty deep and other places we could walk across the creek barefoot because it was really wide and flat and came up to our ankles.

We found a secret pool. We'd lay on the ground and look down into the water. Tiny baby fish-looking things with legs and tails wiggled around in there, and also water spiders with legs that went in and out, in and out, skated across the top.

When it was warm we'd take our clothes off, except for our underwear, and get into the water real slow so not to scare any creatures. I liked it when the little fish nibbled on my toes. It tickled. Sometimes a water snake would swim by us but nothing in the pool ever bit or stung.

Mom didn't know about the pool. Nobody did. By the time we finished running back home we were all dry. First we'd stop in the blackberry patch. It was always real hot in there and the berries are hot too. But the juice was sweet. I liked how it got all purple on my hands and wouldn't wash out.

Then we raced through the grass to the house. Will always won. One time he was way ahead of me and I saw him jump up in the air real high and take off even faster. I almost fell down laughing. Turns out he stepped on a garter snake and it scared him. I bet it scared the snake more. "They won't bother you," Mom always said, "They're good for keeping the mice down."

"Will! Will! Did you see me? Did you see me and Comanche?"

Will threw a rock across the creek so it would skip. "Nah, I been down here."

"Comanche took off with me and it was really scary and we went past
    the salt lick I could barely see it and we almost hit the sheep but
    Uncle Earl came riding up on his horse and threw a rope around
    Comanche's head and pulled us to a stop and then we went back to
    the barn and I held on real good the whole time I never went so fast."

Will laughed. "I sure wish I'd a seen that!"

"So whaddya been doin'?"

"I tried to build a dam over there but it kept washing away."

"You mean like the kind beavers make?"

"Yeah, I guess. But it's too fast and deep right there."

"Does Uncle Earl really drown kittens here?"

"He sure does," said Will. "Puts 'em in a burlap sack, ties it up real tight,
    and lets it sink down in the water till they all die."

"Why does he do that?"

Will shrugged. "I dunno. Guess he don't want any more cats."

I stared at the water, thinking of newborn kittens, still warm, blind,
    mewing for their mama. I held some once and they were really soft.
    And then I thought of Uncle Earl with his big smile and black hair
    and tattoos throwing kittens in a rough sack and dropping them into
    the cold water where they would never get out. He was so much
    bigger than them. I wondered how he could do it.

"Here, I'll drown you!" Will shouted as he grabbed at my braids.

I moved before he could get hold and took off running back to the house.
Will slipped and fell but I kept running. Pretty soon I heard him behind
    me yell, "I'm gonna kill you!"

I screamed as I ran into the house. The front door slammed behind me. I
    kept on full speed into the kitchen and ran headfirst into a big bowl
    of hot gravy Aunt Tootsie was carrying to the table.

The bowl crashed to the floor breaking into several big pieces and I fell
    down with it. Hot gravy went everywhere. On me, my aunt, the floor,

the table, and some even hit my mother who was stirring a pot on the woodstove. Will stood in the doorway acting like Mister Goody-goody. I wished some of the gravy had landed on him.

"Steed Gaulden!" Mom yelled. She came towards me with a wooden spoon in her hand and I burst out crying.

"It's alright," Aunt Tootsie said. She helped me stand up while Mom gave me a mean, hard look.

"Good heavens, Kitty. She's already got a bump on her the size of an egg."

"Ow, that hurts."

"I'll give you something that really hurts if you don't stand still." Mom pulled me away from Aunt Tootsie to check my forehead herself. "That's what you get for running in the house. How many times have I told you?"

"But Mom, Will was chasing me. He was gonna kill me."

Mom smacked me once on the rear-end but it didn't hurt as bad as my head. Will started to laugh until Mom looked at him and then he ran back outside before she could smack him too.

"William dammit, get back here and help clean up this mess!"

He didn't answer or come back.

"That's his middle name," Mom said to herself. "Dammit."

Aunt Tootsie was already picking up the big chunks of yellow that used to be her gravy bowl.

"I'm sorry, Aunt Tootsie," I said and started to cry again.

"It's alright, Sweetie. I bet you won't do that again anytime soon, huh?"

I shook my head which hurt even more. "My head hurts."

"Well, I don't doubt it," Mom snapped. "Tootsie, I've told them a thousand times not to run in the house."

"They're just kids."

"That's no excuse."

"Kitten, you've forgotten what it's like to be a child."

Mom didn't say anything. Aunt Tootsie was older. She had watched Mom grow up and knew all kinds of stuff about her.

"Steed, why don't you go lay down on the couch with Sissy?"

I followed Aunt Tootsie into the living room. She pushed a soft pillow into one corner and I crawled up on the red velvet couch with white fringe around it.

"C'mon, Sissy. Curl up with Steed and make her all better."

As soon as I put my head down on the pillow, the big black-and-white cat came over and did just what Aunt Tootsie said.

"I wanna go to school with Will."

"No, Steed. You have to stay home with me," Mom said.

"How come Will gets to go and I don't?"

"I've told you a hundred times. You have to be five years old to start kindergarten."

"But I am five years old."

"I know. But you weren't five years old in September when school started."

"Well, I almost was. Now I'll be six years old when I'm in kindergarten. It's not fair."

Will stuck his tongue out at me and put on his jacket.

"Shut up, Will!"

"Steed Gaulden, how many times have I told you not to say 'shut up'?"

"Will stuck his tongue out at me," I said.

"I don't care. It's not a nice thing to say to somebody."

Will stuck his tongue out again.

"But Mom..."

"No buts about it. Will, dammit, get going or you'll miss the bus."

Mom turned around to get Will's lunch pail and I stuck my tongue out at him for a long time but he never did look back at me. When the back door slammed behind him I ran to the front room window to watch.

There goes Will. Free from Mom. Free from the house. Free all day long.

Mom wouldn't even let me walk up the road with him. So I had to watch from inside.

Will had on his red wool jacket and his Davy Crockett hat with the tail hanging down the back of his head. I wanted one of those hats too but Mom said we didn't have enough money for two and besides they were only for boys.

The driveway from our house to the road was really, really long and went way up a steep hill to the road. Mom came in and looked out the window to check on how far Will had gone.

"Come help me clean up, Steed. Your dad will be home from work pretty soon and I need to start cooking all over again."

She left the room and I kept my eyes on Will. He was at the top, on the road. A big logging truck went by loaded with Douglas fir trees. I knew what kind they were because Uncle Earl said we lived in Douglas County and that it was named after them.

Will crossed the road and stood on the other side by the big hill to catch the school bus that came from the right. It first went to get the kids that lived way past our place and on the way back to town it stopped for Will, and after that the Murphy kids, and then went into town to the school.

I watched Will pick something up off the road and start swinging it around. Pretty soon he threw it down. The bus came around the bend and stopped. I always watched it drive off and tried to see Will inside the bus but it was too far away. But this time the bus took off and Will was still standing there. He came running down the driveway.

"Mom!" I ran into the kitchen. "Will didn't get on the bus!"

"Don't run in the house, Steed! What did you say?"

"He didn't get on the bus."

Just then Will opened the back door and started to come inside and Mom screamed.

"William dammit!"

"What's wrong?" Will asked, stinking of dead skunk.

"Pewee!" I yelled and held my nose.

"Don't come in this house!" Mom yelled. "Take all those clothes off and leave them on the porch."

"Aw, Mom! It's cold out here."

"That's too damn bad. Hurry up. Good God," Mom said and slammed the door in his face.

"Pewee!" I yelled again.

"Alright, Steed. That's enough. Clear the table while I go get Will some clean clothes."

I went to the back door, opened it a crack, and yelled, "Pewee!" And then
I stuck my tongue out at him and slammed the door.

Mom came stomping back into the kitchen. "Your father's going to be mad,"
Mom said to Will when she tossed his clean clothes out the door.

But me and Will knew that it was a lie. Dad never got mad at us. He
never talked to us either. He left everything up to Mom. I guess that
was because he worked all night on what they call the Graveyard
Shift, which sounded spooky to me. When he wasn't working
or sleeping or eating then he did things like fix the fence or the
chicken coop or take the car to town for oil or put air in the tires.

The back door opened. "Can I come in now?" Will asked. "I'm freezing."

Mom sat down and took a deep breath. She sounded like when you put
a hole in a tire or a balloon. "Get inside here before you catch cold.
That's all I need is for you to get sick and then have Steed catch
it. Then I'd have two sick kids on my hands. Then your father would
probably get it and he'd miss work and next thing you know we're in
the poorhouse."

Will came inside and stood by the woodstove in the kitchen. He never
did take off his Davy Crockett hat.

"Can we go out and play?" I asked. I was really happy Will was going to
be home all day with me.

"Maybe later when it warms up," Mom said. "That is, if it warms up. Will,
you sit down and I'll make some hot chocolate to get the chill out of
your bones. Steed, clear off that table like I asked you an hour ago."

"Don't I get any hot chocolate?"

"Not if you don't hurry up and do what I say."

So I did.

———————

Dad came home and the first thing he said was, "What in the hell happened?"
He had to walk past Will's skunked-up clothes out on the back porch.

Me and Will started giggling.

"Pewee!" I yelled, holding my nose.

Mom looked at me and shook her head. "Will, take your sister and go in the front room. You can play quietly. But I don't want to hear another peep out of either one of you, do you hear me?"

We spread out plain paper on the front room floor and I got my crayons and colored pencils and Will and I drew pictures while we listened.

"Those kids are going to drive me crazy, Bruce."

"Well, what happened?"

"Will apparently found a dead skunk up there on the road and played with it before the bus came."

"That explains the stinky clothes outside," Dad said.

"Then the bus came. Can't you just see Jenny's face when she opened the bus door to let him in?" Mom actually laughed a little. So did Dad.

I looked at Will and he smiled real big.

"So anyway," Mom continued, "no school for Will today. And I'll probably have to burn those clothes. I don't want to put them in the washing machine. And I'm sure as hell not going to wash them by hand. That means having to buy another pair of jeans for him. He's got enough shirts and socks. But that leaves him with only one pair of jeans."

I could hear Dad pull a chair out from the table and sit down. "How much does that cost?" he asked.

"Plenty," Mom said.

I looked at Will. He didn't smile this time.

"Kitty, I don't get paid until Friday."

"I know that. We should be alright till then. As long as he doesn't ruin the pair he's got on now. As it is, I've patched and patched them."

I kept coloring a bigger and bigger sun on my paper.

"What's for supper?" Dad asked. Since he worked nights, he ate supper in the morning when he got home, which seemed so funny to me. And before he went to work, he ate breakfast at night.

Mom started banging pots and pans around getting ready to fry up potatoes and onions.

"Hamburger okay with you?" she asked.

"That'll be fine."

"I was planning on making a meatloaf this morning in time for you to
    have some but you can thank Will for the fact I never got to it."
Will scribbled his sky all blue and black. And then he put some smoke
    coming out of the fireplace on the house he drew.
"Hamburger's fine. Is there a beer in the refrigerator?"
Mom got it for him and kept on cooking. Just smelling the food made
    me hungry even though it wasn't anywhere near lunchtime. I went
    to the kitchen.
"Mom, can we go out and play now?"
"Steed, what did I tell you? I don't want to hear a peep out of you until I say so."
I looked at Dad and he winked at me. He did that a lot and I wanted to
    ask Mom why Dad winked at me but I didn't want to get yelled at.
"I'm hungry." I tried not to say it but it just came out.
Mom whirled around, grabbed my arm, and whacked me on the rear-end
    with the wooden spoon in her hand. "Get out of the kitchen until I
    call you. When your father is through eating, he's going to bed. And
    then you can help me clean up this kitchen. Now get."
I ran back into the front room.
Will stuck his tongue out at me and I stuck mine out at him. He did it
    again. So I did it again. Then he tried to tickle me but I pushed him
    away. Then he took the crayon I was using. So I got a new one. He
    pulled that one out of my hand. I started to get another one but he
    grabbed the whole box and ran down the hall.
"Mom!" I screamed. She came running into the room. "Will took all the
    crayons! He won't let me color!"
"Go to your room!" Mom screamed back.
"But I didn't do anything." I started crying.
"Steed Gaulden, one more sound out of you and I will give you something
    to cry about."
I walked slowly out of the room.
"William dammit, get in here!"
Will passed me in the hall. I stuck my tongue out at him and he slugged
    me in the arm.

"You're walking on thin ice, Mister!" I heard Mom yell, followed by three whacks as she smacked his rear-end with the same wooden spoon.

Will came back down the hall looking real sad. I was waiting for him. "Can I read your schoolbooks?" I asked.

"Sure," he said. "I'll help you."

I followed him into his room. He gave me a book about Indians and I tried real hard to read it.

"I'm tired, Will. I wanna read my books now." I went into my room and got one of my Little Golden Books called Busy Timmy and ran back to his room. "I like this one. Mom said if I had been a boy they were gonna name me Timmy."

"I'll call you Timmy if you want," Will said.

"No, that's okay." I opened the book.

"'Timmy is a big boy'," I read out loud all by myself. "'He can put on his outdoor—what's this word?"

Will looked at the page of the little boy getting dressed. "Clothes," he said.

"Oh yeah." I was going to say cloth. "'He can find his shovel and his big sand pail.'" I turned the page.

"'He goes down the steps. No one has to help him. He's a big boy now.'"

I flipped through the book looking at the drawings of Timmy and the rabbit and the squirrel and the robin and his shovel and pail and him in the bathtub and him asleep.

"Are you done?" Will asked.

"Wait. I wanna read the last page." I flipped to the back of the book. "Listen, Will. I can read every word all by myself."

"Then do it."

"'You are big, too. Timmy does a lot of things. So can you!'" I tossed the book on Will's bed. "And I can! I can do anything I want!" I yelled.

Mom came down the hall and we both sat there not saying anything.

"Your father's gone to bed so you kids go outside now and play."

"Yippee!" I yelled.

"Shhh, Steed. Be quiet. Didn't I just say your dad's trying to sleep?"

Will and I both jumped up and ran to the kitchen to get our jackets. Will still had his Davy Crockett hat on.

I put on the wool cap Aunt Frankie sent me for Christmas. Aunt Frankie
like Aunt Tootsie was my grandma's sister.

"Stay close," Mom said. "And don't make a bunch of noise."

We burst out the back door.

"I'll call you when it's time for lunch" Mom said, grabbing the door before
it slammed.

"Pewee!" I yelled as I jumped over Will's stinky clothes.

"Steed. Be quiet," Mom said behind me in a low voice.

Will took off towards the barn and I ran after him.

"I sure am glad you had to stay home today," I said when we reached
the barn.

"Let's look for eggs," Will said.

I liked how the barn smells. Even when it was cold out, the barn smelled
warm just like when I crawled under a big blanket with Aunt
Tootsie's cat, Sissy, or the dog we used to have.

The chicken coop was halfways inside and halfways outside. Inside the
barn there was a wood door with a little piece of wood nailed to it
for a handle. You turned it up to open or straight to close it. The door
went into the place where the chickens laid their eggs. It was even
warmer in there.

"Let me open the door!" I called to Will.

"Well, c'mon then!"

I turned the smooth piece of wood real slow and we went in on tiptoe.
Will first, then me. Some of the chickens still ran out into their yard.
But most of them stayed on their nests.

"Be quiet, Steed."

"Okay," I whispered.

I started checking the nests at the bottom. Will always checked the ones
up higher because he could reach them. A couple of chickens got
up real slow and grumbled at us when we got close to them. One
jumped down and I put my hand on the hay that was all pushed
down and smooth and warm where she had just sat. There was a
big, warm brown egg, almost as big as my hand.

"Look, Will," I whispered, and held the egg up for him to see.

"Good one. Put it in the basket over there. And be careful."

"I will." I carried it in both hands to the basket hanging near the door. Will had already put three brown eggs in there. But mine was the biggest.

"That's all for now," Will said. "I can't find any more."

"Let me look one more time."

"Okay."

I went from nest to nest. A couple chickens still didn't move. "You're right. That's all there is."

"We'd better take them to the house."

"Let me carry them."

"Better be careful or Mom will get really mad at you."

"I will," I promised.

I took the basket by the handle. Four eggs don't make it very heavy, but they were rolling around so I put my hand in the basket to hold them still. "Open the door, Will."

He let me out of the coop and I walked so slow to the house I thought I would never get there. I looked back but Will was nowhere to be seen. I hope he didn't go down to the creek without me. I made it to the back porch and set the basket down. I looked back again for Will but I didn't see or hear anything.

"Mom," I said real quiet. I opened the back door. "Mom?"

She wasn't in the kitchen so I took the basket and went inside and set it on the table. I wanted to go back outside but I had to go to the bathroom. I knew Will was long gone by now and I felt like crying because I didn't like to go down to the creek without him and he never wanted to wait for me. I started down the hall to the bathroom when I heard some funny noises. They came from Mom and Dad's room. It didn't sound like them but I couldn't figure out who else could be in their room. I went inside the bathroom and closed the door. When I came out, Mom was coming out of their bedroom. I guess she didn't know I was in the house because she almost screamed when she saw me.

"How long have you been here?" she asked.

"Not very long. I had to go to the bathroom."

"You scared me to death, Steed. Where's Will?"

"I think he went down to the creek."

"Well, don't go sneaking around like that."

"Is Dad okay?"

"Of course, why shouldn't he be?"

"I thought he was sleeping."

"Is that you out there, Steed?" he called from the bedroom.

Mom looked at me. "Now see what you've done?"

"Kitty, let her come in for awhile."

Mom opened the bedroom door and pushed me inside. Dad was in bed
with the covers over him, smoking a cigarette.

"Don't keep your father awake too long," Mom said and closed the door
behind me. I heard her walk back up the hall to the kitchen.

C'mere, kid," Dad said and winked at me.

"I'm...I'm kinda dirty, Dad."

"Get over here."

"But I've been in the barn with the chickens."

"Just come over here for a minute."

I started to walk over to the other side of the bed but he stopped me.

"Steed. Over here."

"Yes...sir."

He put his cigarette out in the ashtray on the nightstand. There were a
few butts in it and two had lipstick on them. Mom only wore lipstick
when she went to town or when Dad was home.

"You don't look so dirty to me."

I stood still. He pulled me close to his face.

"You smell like cigarettes," I said.

Dad laughed.

"And beer."

"That's not so bad. That's what a man is supposed to smell like."

I wrinkled my nose but I didn't say anything.

"Gimme a kiss."

"Dad," I tried pulling away. "Will's waiting for me to go down to the creek."

"Will can wait." With that he put his hand on the back of my head and forced my face up against his. His chin was scratchy with whiskers.

"Dad," I started to yell and he put his tongue in my mouth and dragged me into the bed. I couldn't breathe or scream or do anything. I remembered how he winked at me. With his other hand he pulled my jeans down to my shoes and pulled down my panties. I couldn't make a sound with his tongue in my mouth. I couldn't breathe. I started to choke. He pushed his hand up between my legs and shoved a finger deep inside me. I started to cry and choke so he took his tongue out of my mouth.

"Don't you make a sound. Not one sound, Steed. I won't hurt you. You'll see. You'll like it. Shhhh. Be quiet. That's a girl. Be quiet."

I closed my eyes and stuffed the blanket in my mouth while he kept going in and out with his finger and then pretty soon I felt something softer and warmer and wetter. It didn't hurt but his whiskers rubbed hard against my legs. Dad made a humming sound and then everything ended and he rolled off me.

"Remember, don't you tell your mother. Do you hear me?"

I pulled my panties and jeans back up and jumped out the other side of the bed.

"I mean it, Steed. If you tell anyone you'll be sorry. It's our little secret, okay?"

As I ran out the door I heard him say, "Remember. Be quiet."

I not only kept quiet, I blocked it completely out of my mind.

19

"You're a sad and angry person," the therapist said matter-of-factly.
Immediately I felt sad although there was no judgment in his voice. Nor
    compassion either.
He could have been telling me I had a nail in my tire, but the impassive
    words punctured my consciousness. At first I was deflated.
Then I got angry—at least inside.
How dare he say such a thing. He doesn't even know me. I didn't come
    here to be criticized or insulted or to have my feelings hurt. I was
    already hurting before coming here. Can't he see that? What kind of
    therapist is he anyhow?
Maybe it was because I wasn't a full-paying client.
The local agency offered counseling on a sliding scale, and I slid in near
    the bottom to get help.
My life now closed in on me even more. It was worse than having
    blinders on. It was more like going blind. I did my best to maintain
    my composure as I formulated my response.
"Steve and I have been married more than a year. We lived together a year
    before that. And in all that time we had sex maybe twenty times. He
    wanted it. I didn't. Something is wrong. Very, very wrong. And it isn't
    getting better."
The therapist just let me talk. I wasn't one hundred percent sure he was
    listening, but I talked anyway.

"The pressure on me builds as each day passes. He never lets me forget
that he wants sex, that he is ready, any time, just say the word, and he'll
drop his pants."

"Just like that," the therapist stated

"Just like that," I replied.

"So easy."

"Not for me," I said. "So I started sleeping ten, eleven, even twelve hours a night.
I cannot stay awake past nine p.m. I excuse myself from him in the living
room, fire burning in the woodstove, TV going, and head to the safety
of Sleepsville. There, no one touches me. No one demands or expects
anything from me. Especially myself."

"What do you expect of yourself?"

"My constant self-inquiry of why, why, why am I this way, what is wrong with
me, what am I to do? gets shut down for the night."

"And then?" he asked.

"The next morning I force myself to get up and start all over again."

I even went to the library and looked up whatever I could find that might
describe my problem. My problem, mind you. I came across 'frigidity.'
That halfway sounded like a possible explanation. I went right home and
announced to Steve that I must be frigid. He happily agreed. Now we
had a name for my problem and we could both now work on fixing me.

But the tension kept building between us even though we make good
companions cooking up great meals in the kitchen or sitting on the deck
drinking gin & tonics. Or especially sharing our work.

He shows me his latest photograph and I share my latest poem.

"We can talk non-stop all day long and into the night about every topic under
the sun. But I cannot bring myself to have sex with him. It would be
easier for me to swim across the ocean than to walk across the room
and jump in bed with him."

So what was wrong with me?

I looked at the therapist. He was a blur beyond the tears that ran down my face.

"Where is your husband?" he asked.

The question shocked me. Wasn't it already obvious after what I told him that I was the one who is messed up?

"He said this is my problem. I must be frigid," I answered in all seriousness.

The man laughed.

I wiped away at the tears, trying hard to blink him into focus again.

"Why is that funny?"

He smiled at me in a genuinely kind way. "It takes two," he said.

I began to sob and sob. The previous tears were nothing like what poured out of me then.

The man waited patiently.

"He won't go to therapy," I finally managed to say.

The therapist shrugged his shoulders.

My heart folded in on itself. "Does this mean you won't help me if I come by myself?"

"No, of course not. I'll help you."

I took a breath.

"But it does mean that you will change and your husband won't," he explained.

Deflated, I drove home as slowly as possible through Eureka, a town on the North Coast of California. I felt as gray and thick as the fog that holds the town captive most of the year.

Slowly I drove, out past grazing brown cows accompanied by white egrets in the soggy pasture and past the little store in Freshwater where loggers went for their beer and tobacco, wearing slippers on their aching feet after spending grueling hours on slippery wet slopes cutting down one hundred-year-old redwoods. Then I slowly drove up the redwood-covered hill towards Kneeland, a spot in the road with a post office, a pay phone, and miles further out, a one-room schoolhouse where redneck ranchers send their children.

Halfway up the hill, I emerged from the fog.

From the deck on our ten acres you can see Trinidad Head way off in the distance marking where the coastline meets the horizon.

That is, if it isn't socked in with fog.

We live on the side of a mountain like the cartoon character, Snuffy Smith. Our house is a doublewide trailer.

The previous owner propped it on pier and beams and tall pilings so it resembles a ship half launched into space. He added an enclosed porch the full length of the trailer and put a pitched metal roof over the entire structure.

When it rains, which it does nearly every hour of every day, or so it seems, the porch vibrates with thunderous pounding. So loud, in fact, you have to yell at each other to be heard.

Entering the front door of the porch, you have to go all the way down to the other end of the porch where a sliding glass door opens into the trailer. Or you can go straight out the French door onto a massive deck protruding high above the ground.

When I slid the glass door open and went inside I could see that Steve had been anxiously waiting just by the look on his face.

"Well, what happened? How'd it go? What did he say?"

His battering of questions told me he was more worried about himself than what happened to me or how I did. For an instant he seemed worried he'd been found out, but I could not get my mind around what it could possibly mean. Then there was a clap of thunder and I lost sight of it and wouldn't get another glimpse for almost a decade.

The machine-gun questioning continued.

I felt numb.

Finally he paused.

I spoke.

"The therapist asked me why you weren't there."

"What? Why?"

He was convinced I was the one with a problem. So was I. "He said it takes two," I said.

Steve jumped up.

"Sheeiit," he sneered angrily.

This was something he hadn't counted on.

"Does that mean you won't go for counseling?" I asked.

"I don't need that shit."

He paced like a caged animal — wild, full of fear, and angry.

I watched him, amazed.

"I'm not going."

"Fine," I sighed.

"Really?"

"Yeah, I'll go by myself."

He looked at me.

"But," I added, "I will change and you won't."

For some reason that stopped him cold. "What are you talking about?" he challenged.

"That's what the therapist said. I will change and you won't."

"He said that?"

"Yep."

Silence.

"I don't want that to happen," he mumbled.

I shrugged. Deep down it already had.

Weeks passed.

Every time I brought up the subject of making an appointment there was the usual excuse that we didn't have enough money. Sliding scale or no sliding scale.

Finally I dropped the subject altogether.

We had formed a silent pact.

Steve let up on pressuring me to have sex whenever he wanted it.

I never mentioned therapy again.

We coasted.

Months passed.

But the reality remained like an enormous beast in the center of our home that kept getting bigger and bigger as we kept walking around it and avoiding it, trying to pretend it wasn't there.

The pressure returned.

My misery and despair intensified. I felt like a freak, and very alone. Avoiding the topic only seemed to nurture the beast until it consumed us both.

Together we decided whatever problems we had could surely be resolved by devoting ourselves to a spiritual practice.

20

Steve and I both were seekers long before we met, so it seemed natural for
  us to turn to religion for the answer.

He had been into Zen Buddhism for a few years off and on, first in L.A. and
  then San Francisco where he was living when we met.

Though I was still in high school, my exposure to various religions continued
  to expand, thanks to the Sixties.

As long as I can remember, I'd been searching.

When I was in fourth grade, our class made a papier-mâché model of a
  Hopi Indian village. I fell in love with the Hopis and anything American
  Indian. From then on, exotic or foreign people and cultures held great
  attraction for me.

I longed to escape my world and the life I led, though I had no clue why.

Advertisements in various magazines that came to our house offered free
  travel booklets and maps to various places throughout the United States
  and Canada. I wrote away for brochures.. I dreamt of running away to all
  of them. They looked so much prettier than where I lived, mountains and
  rivers and green hills with big trees while we lived in a tract development
  of houses that all looked the same with black asphalt streets, gray
  cement sidewalks, street lights, and a patch of grass in everyone's front
  yard. At the end of my street, tumbleweeds blew across the school fields
  and tangled with the chain link fence.

By age 14 on, I had read everything I could get my hands on. I had also started writing poetry exclusively.

I inhaled Rabindrinath Tagore, American Indian philosophies, Lao-Tzu, and Japanese haiku. I took World Literature in my senior year. I fell in love with Emily Dickinson and Edna St. Vincent Millay. I read about Hinduism and Buddhism.

I tried teaching myself how to do yoga. I'd even tried teaching myself to meditate by lighting a candle and concentrating on a flower. That didn't work too well. My mind would not stop wandering.

Occasionally I accompanied a friend to Catholic Mass on Sunday. I did all this in Anaheim, home of Disneyland, in conservative Orange County, California where I attended Walt Disney Elementary School.

When I was in high school my mother gave me her Bible. The very word "bible" was never mentioned nor was the book ever read in our house while I was growing up.

She and my father had taken me and my brother to the Episcopal Church when we lived in Myrtle Creek, Oregon. That must have been where her Bible came from. After only a year, my father lost his job (or maybe he quit, but Mom would never tell us that), so we moved back to Southern California. There, churchgoing slowly diminished from the occasional Sunday to Easter and Christmas then finally disappeared altogether.

Grandma-Great was the only one in the family who attended church. She and my great-grandfather had been devout Methodists. He died long before I was born. But my mother knew him all during her childhood and up until she married. Grandma-Great was Kittie Clock, mother of my mother's father. He died when my mother was a baby.

We saw Grandma-Great at Christmas and maybe one other time during the year. So there wasn't much chance for her to influence us kids. I think my father wanted it that way. He never acted real warm towards her, or towards any of the family other than his own brother and sister, my Uncle Tom and Aunt Jeanne.

I started reading Mom's Bible after I went to a Holy Roller church with

Donny Deward, a friend and fellow dope-smoker. I don't know what it was about that church but I ended up speaking in tongues one afternoon with a group of believers gathered around me. I could hear myself babbling away but did not understand one word. It sounded ancient, like what hieroglyphics might sound like if put to music.

During that brief period, I underlined most of the Bible passages with a red pen. I don't recollect why. Anyway, after speaking in tongues, I never went back. I didn't like having all those people around me when I was in another state. It reminded me of the movie, *Rosemary's Baby.*

Besides, Eastern religions made more sense to me. They are based on having an experience within oneself. Realizing one's true nature. That God dwells within you, as you, and not living in a castle up in the clouds separate from you. Nature plays a huge part as well. Both of those aspects appealed to me. So when the Zen shoe fit, I decided to wear it.

It was the religion of choice ever since I'd met Steve and he thrust a book at me declaring, "Here's where I'm at."

The book was a well-worn copy of *The Three Pillars of Zen.* I was ripe and ready. I couldn't put it down.

Are you goin' to San Francisco?

Don't forget to wear some flowers in your hair like the song says.

At that time, Steve lived in San Francisco just over the hill from Haight-Ashbury.

I'd flown up for the weekend to visit Deanna, a girlfriend from high school. She had dropped out of school months before and headed north. Next thing I knew she was writing me from the Bay Area to come visit her. It was my first airplane trip. I was 18.

Deanna met me at the airport.

Tall, long straight blonde hair, wide hips, small breasts, and always attracting men. It made me uncomfortable.

"I wanted to wait till you got here to tell you about Ari."

"What?" I was instantly worried. Whenever a guy entered the picture with Deanna, I worried because things usually grew more complicated by the hour.

"I met him hitchhiking. I was trying to get back over the bridge to Oakland

and so was he and so we got to talking and finally we hitched a ride
together. And I've been living with him ever since."

Shivers went up my spine. I just didn't know how she could do it. How she
could just meet a guy and within an hour or a day, be naked and doing
God-knows-what with him. Or him doing God-knows what to her.

Deanna had been sleeping with guys since she was 15. And even
though I ran around with her, I happened to still be a virgin.

She treated sex like it was no big thing. I was in awe how relaxed she
was about it. Like it was totally natural. To me, death was preferable
over sex. And I was terrified of dying.

"Ari's really far out," she exclaimed as she drove us onto the freeway in an
old Peugeot.

"Isn't this a bitchen car? It belongs to Ari's friends. We're house-sitting for
them in Piedmont. They went to Europe for three months. Wait'll you
see the place! And I can't wait for you to meet Ari. Oh yeah, and his
best friend, Steve, wants to meet you."

I stopped breathing. "Oh no. No guys. No. Nope. Don't want to meet any
guys. I'm going to France in March. I don't want to meet anybody!"

She looked at me with concern. "Okay, okay. So I won't call him."

"Anyway, why does he want to meet me?"

"I showed him pictures of you. Remember the ones we took at your house
that day we got so stoned? And we got up on the roof! And that one
of you in the shower holding the big flower! Those were great."

"Well, I don't want to meet him." I still couldn't breathe.

"Okay, then."

She took the next exit off the freeway, plunging us into the depths of
San Francisco.

"He asked me to call him when you got here and I just won't."

"Good. Now…look what I brought."

"Holy shit!" Deanna yelled.

I held two purple tumblers of LSD in the palm of my hand. In those days
you could carry a ticking bomb onto a plane and no one searched you.

"Yeah, I scored them from Phil. Remember him? I told him I was gonna see you and he got these especially for us."

"Far out!!!!"

"He didn't charge me much either."

The day was young. Deanna parked the Peugeot near Golden Gate Park and we each took a purple tumbler into our mouths and swallowed.

"C'mon! Let's go get some fish and chips! It's a really good place."

Mostly long-haired guys and hippie chicks jammed the place waiting for hot fried fish with French fries served on butcher paper and doused with salt and vinegar.

The acid was already coming on.

We spent the whole day tripping around Haight Ashbury (known locally as "the Haight") and meandered in and out of Golden Gate Park taking pictures of each other darting among the bushes. Talk about blowing it. I'm sure it was quite obvious to others we were ripped. But we didn't have to worry about it or get paranoid because everybody else was either stoned or just digging it.

People hung out everywhere. On the streets, in shops, in the park smoking grass, playing music, dancing, tripping, laughing, sitting in circles talking, passing joints around, sharing food, sharing kisses, hugs, you name it.

Further down the Haight, a health food store occupied a tiny corner shop. It was crammed with bins and tubs and barrels of bulk whole wheat flour, brown rice, bulgur wheat, oats, barley, millet, and soybeans. No glamour, shiny wrappers, fluff, advertising, or fancy signage. Just handwritten prices and names of products on 3x5 cards clipped near each item. I'd never seen anything like it. Everybody brought their own containers to buy cold-pressed cooking oils, peanut butter, almond butter, honey, tofu, yogurt, soy sauce, cheeses, raisins, pumpkin seeds, homemade soap, and biodegradable detergents. There were a few packaged goods such as Dr. Bronner's Sesame Chips, Paul Bragg's Apple Cider Vinegar, Hain's Sea Salt, and imported Virgin Olive Oil.

Shops along the Haight overflowed with festive handmade goods. Tie-dyed T-shirts, batik dresses and scarves, colorful crocheted berets, leather sandals and belts, hammered silver earrings and beaded necklaces,

woven sashes and shawls, quilted coats and Levi jackets covered in
appliqués or miniature American flags, handmade candles, rose-
colored sunglasses with round lenses rimmed in wire. Incense
burned constantly in every store. Jumbo Classic Champa from
Indian ashrams and short Joss sticks such as the kind used in Zen
and other Buddhist temples. Body oils added to the mix of aromas.
My choice was Patchouli.

A cacophony of music, people, babies, dogs, color, and movement
reverberated.

And flowers everywhere.

Psychedelic posters in shop windows and stapled to telephone poles
advertised performances by Big Brother & the Holding Company,
the Grateful Dead, Ravi Shankar, Country Joe & the Fish, The Who,
The Doors, Jefferson Airplane. There were record stores selling all
the latest records, James Taylor, 96 Tears, next to the first and only
brown rice-and-vegetables take out stand, stacks of used, worn
Levis for sale, The Fillmore; free love. Everywhere hung brass bells
on leather cords to tie around your wrist or ankle…or both, hand-
thrown pottery, glass wind chimes, hanging plants in macramé
holders (the art of knot tying), Black is black, ribbons with delicate
bells to weave through your hair, lace blouses, no bras, long full
skirts, bell bottoms, guys with ponytails, braids, tambourines, African
drums, flutes and recorders, guitars—acoustic and electric, music
and marijuana wafting in the air everywhere with pungent hashish
jumping in every now and then like a tenor sax.

This is the dawning of the Age of Aquarius.

Books, books, and more books, and newspapers and magazines, and
strong coffee in crowded coffeehouses filled with discussions
of politics, philosophy, religion, the search for meaning in life, the
ongoing Vietnam War, scientific, psychic, and planetary possibilities…
while others sat alone writing poetry, stories, songs, letters,
dissertations, editorials, daily journals, or strumming a guitar, reading
a book or the Berkeley Barb or the San Francisco Chronicle. Dodge

the Draft, vegetarian, Sufi, Rinzai-Zen, Hare Krishna, the Free Speech Movement, Soto Zen, long hair, beards, grow your own food, macrobiotic, Tao-te-Ching, Tibetan Book of the Dead, grow your own stash, hash pipes, roach clips, Arlo Guthrie, Indian madras bedspreads, Chinese herbs, friendly strangers, strange friends, Procol Harum, Mother Earth, earth mothers with squabbles of hippie kids happy, free, and barefoot; bare breasts swinging under sheer peasant blouses with embroidery on the sleeves, acid rock, Bob Dylan, a psychedelic poster of Dylan's profile, Donovan, Electric Flag, the Beatles, Sergeant Pepper's Lonely Hearts Club Band, George Harrison, My Sweet Lord… The assassination of President Kennedy, climbing the Himalayas, transcendental meditation, ashram, zendo, yoga, Tai Chi, bancha tea, Canned Heat, VW buses, the Rolling Stones, sexual revolution, women with unshaven legs and armpits, Lucy in the Sky with Diamonds, communes, the I Ching, two-finger V peace sign, Aretha Franklin, meditation zafu and zabuton, prayer shawl, prayer flags, Jews for Jesus, jeans and boots, drawstring pants, moccasins, American Indians… John Mayall, Wild Thing, B.B. King, strobe lights and the Shrine, I Can't Get No Satisfaction, wild free-form dancing, the Golden Bear, Paul Butterfield and the Blues Band, bodysurfing, Beach Boulevard, the Wedge, Jack Kerouac, hitchhiking, Love-Ins, Buffy Saint-Marie, Twiggy, Marianne Faithful, Mary Quant, Tune In Turn On Drop Out, back to the land, Om, chop wood carry water, Tassajara, Big Sur, What Is the Sound of One Hand Clapping?, Esalen, Joni Mitchell, Judy Collins, Carly Simon, Simon & Garfunkle… Make Love Not War, Sun Ra, Patty Waters, Yusef Lateef, Save Water Shower With A Friend, You can get anything you want at Alice's restaurant, Black Panthers, Afros, Terry Riley, Malcolm X, John Fahey, Peter Paul & Mary, Joan Baez, Pete Seeger, Timothy Leary, Dave Clark Five, The Mamas & the Papas, One Flew Over the Cuckoo's Nest, Dusty Springfield, Carole King, natural childbirth, make your own yogurt, make your own bread, make your own baby food, make your own clothes, make your own house… 100% cotton, Farmers Market, I see a bad moon rising, the Silent Majority, color color everywhere, Magical Mystery Tour, Black Is

Beautiful, Save the Redwoods, Happiness is a Warm Puppy, The Lovin' Spoonful, raw milk, kefir, Adele Davis, bitchen, People's Park, community gardens, zero population growth, Janis Joplin, birth control pills, Santana, hip or straight, narcs, Summerfield, Antonin Artaud, Edgar Cayce, free clinics, R. Crumb's Mr. Natural, head shops, the Byrds, live in a barn, abandoned church, old creamery, school bus, granary, or build a tree house in the redwoods, Andy Warhol, Johnny Carson, stained glass, recycled materials, save a tree, love beads, The Kinks… Moody Blues, Jimi Hendrix, Linda Ronstadt, zig-zags, groovy, nirvana, Easy Rider, take a toke, enlightenment, Baba Ram Dass, Baba Muktananda, meditation revolution, Euell Gibbons, 7-day fast, don't sell out, Led Zeppelin, flashback, Brave New World, Big Brother, Gualala, Mendocino, Sea Ranch, the Zombies, anti-war demonstrations, Gary Burton & the Animals, opium from Nam, midwives, home births, Planned Parenthood, The Cream, blown glass, blown away, blow your mind, Jerry Brown for Governor of California, sculpture, paintings, Salvador Dali, woven wall hangings, rug hooking, Penelope Tree… Give Peace A Chance, Stop In The Name of Love, est, primal scream, Beach Boys, hang ten, Steppenwolf, Time Won't Let Me, the British Invasion, The Graduate, Muhammed Ali, Joe Cocker, counterculture, Cesar Chavez, Laugh-In, Bill Graham, Martin Luther King, Jr., Ken Kesey & The Merry Pranksters, PEACE, far out. And that was just one trip.

21

I had just graduated from high school with an almost 4.0 grade point average in spite of all the sex, drugs, and rock-and-roll. Minus the sex, that is. At eighteen—almost nineteen—I was still a virgin.

Deanna and I were still high on acid when we decided to head back to Piedmont before dark. She managed to maneuver us out of San Francisco in the old Peugeot. We went across the Bay Bridge, into the hills of Piedmont, and up the steep driveway to the stucco house with big bay windows where she and Ari were staying.

"This is it," Deanna said, getting out of the car.

"Nice place. Nice view."

Everywhere I looked were hills covered with trees and pretty houses and in the far distance the very blue San Francisco Bay.

"C'mon, I'll show you where you can crash. It's the kids' room. They've got two boys and a girl. We've been using the boys' room for guests. There's twin beds. Hope that's alright."

"Sure."

I put my suitcase on one bed figuring I would sleep on the other. That is, if I ever come down from the acid.

"Man, I'm still tripping," I said.

"Really? I'm pretty much down," Deanna replied.

"No way!"

"Why don't you just hang out and I'll get us something cold to drink. Aren't you thirsty? I'm dying of thirst. Must've been those fish and chips."

I went into the den that opened off the living room and plopped down in a rocking chair that faced the television. My body was still but my mind was having none of it.

I stretched out my legs and put my feet on the footstool and slowly rocked back and forth, back and forth. That comforted my stoned self.

Deanna came in. "Here, have a beer."

"Thanks," I said. I never drank. Alcohol wasn't my thing, but I took a sip.

She turned on the color TV which instantly mesmerized me. My mom and I still had a black-and-white one at home.

"Guess what? Ari left me a note that Steve came by after all. They went to see a flick."

"Oh no. So now I'm gonna have to meet him?"

"Sorry."

"Maybe we'll be in bed by the time they get home."

"Maybe. And maybe not. Hey, I really like your jeans."

"Bitchen, aren't they?"

We both admired the flower-covered brown denim pants I had on.

"They're so tight they barely go over my boots."

Deanna and I sat there for five minutes or five hours. I have no idea.

There was some noise in the living room and I turned to look.

One of the vertical windows alongside the front door opened and two guys stepped through into the living room. The first one was average height and build with a long black ponytail and full beard. The second guy was the same size and coloring but his hair came to his collar and he had a mustache.

I really liked how he looked in his blue workshirt, sleeves rolled up, Levis, and cowboy boots. What took you so long? I felt like asking him. It's like we made an ancient pact in another life to meet up again. I've been waiting for you for more than a lifetime.

I turned back around and stared at the TV.

"Hi Honey," Deanna said.

"Hey Babe. I forgot my key," said Ari. "That's why we came through the window."

"How was the movie?"

"Good. We saw *The Swimmer* with Burt Lancaster. It was really heavy."

"My friend Steed is here. She brought some acid and we tripped all day in Golden Gate Park. C'mon and meet her."

All three walked into the den where I sat rocking.

"Ari and Steve, this is Steed."

"Hello," I said and kept rocking.

"She's still coming down," Deanna said.

"Welcome," Ari said.

"Thanks."

"Hey Babe, we're hungry. Anything to eat?"

"You could make some sandwiches or there's eggs."

Steve and Ari went into the kitchen and next thing I knew, they were sitting with Deanna and me with a plate of sandwiches.

So we all ate. Two Jewish boys from Pasadena with college degrees from Berkeley and two blonde chicks from Orange County, one a high school dropout and me, the ink barely dry on my high school diploma. I had certainly never met anyone like them before. Deanna had told me earlier that Ari, 28, was a social worker and Steve, 27, was an architect.

Ari and Deanna excused themselves and went to bed, leaving me alone with Steve.

I'm not so sure I like this idea. My mind seemed more clear now.

"I just got back from Oregon," Steve said.

"Really? I lived there when I was little."

"No kidding? Where?"

"Myrtle Creek. It's in Douglas County."

"Douglas County! That is so far out! That's exactly where I was."

"Why were you there?"

"I had a week off work so I went up there to take photographs."

"For what? I thought you were an architect."

"I am. But I really want to get into photography. My dad gave me his old camera so I've just been trying it out."

"I loved Oregon," I said.

"So did I."

We looked at each other and both liked what we saw. And so we talked on and on until four in the morning about Oregon, traveling in general, living in the country versus the city, the importance of smoking grass and taking acid, his photography, my poetry, and my plan to go live in France in the Spring.

"I think I'll just stay since it's so late," Steve said. "There's an extra bed in your room. Do you mind?"

I stopped breathing. "No, I don't mind."

I went into the bathroom and put my Shorty pajamas on. When I came out Steve was sitting on the edge of the other bed with no shirt on. My suitcase now sat on the floor at the foot of the bed. Oh my God. He's half naked already. His chest is covered with hair. He's a man. Not a blond, bare-chested surfer boy like the guys I know. I jumped into my bed and pulled the covers over me all the way to my chin.

"Goodnight," I said.

"Would you like to sleep with me?" Steve asked.

"Uh...no. Thanks. No, I don't."

"Okay." Steve walked over and turned off the overhead light and then got in his bed.

As soon as I closed my eyes I started to panic.

"Steve?"

"Yeah?"

"Would you talk to me for awhile? I guess I'm still coming down from the acid."

"Sure."

"I hope you don't mind that I don't want to sleep with you."

I couldn't tell him I'm a virgin and I'm scared shitless.

"Not at all. Now just close your eyes and take a deep breath. Let it out real slow."

I did. I could hear him breathing in deeply along with me.

"Now focus on your toes. Keep your eyes closed. And imagine a calming energy entering the bottom of your feet and toes. And watch how it moves slowly up your legs…First your ankles…then your calves…and knees…your thighs…just relaxing…and then to your stomach…and your chest. Keep breathing. Let your arms and shoulders relax, your neck, your face and…"

Apparently I dropped off to sleep because I woke up at eleven with the sun burning through the window. I could hear the others in the kitchen so I scrambled out of bed, took a quick shower, and got dressed in the same clothes I had on the day before.

I hurried to the kitchen.

"Good morning," Deanna said. "Heard you two were up all night talking."

I tried not to blush.

"Let's go over to Berkeley to Tilden Park," Steve said. "We can take some food and just hang out."

"You two go," Ari said. "Deanna and I need to do some stuff."

"Are you sure?" I asked, looking at Deanna. "After all, I flew up to visit you and I'm going home tomorrow."

She grinned. "Go on. Have fun. It's a beautiful park. And it's a beautiful day."

And it was.

———·•·———

Steve and I left in his Volkswagen with a bag of tortilla chips, hunks of cheese, and two apples. When we got there, he parked the car and leaned over and kissed me real quick. We walked around the park holding hands or my arm through his. I never once gave any thought to my plans of going to Europe.

"The air feels cooler and the sun feels warmer here," I said. "The sky looks bluer too. Different than Anaheim."

Steve climbed up into a tree with a V-shaped trunk and pulled me up behind him. We sat there, arms around each other. And then we kissed. Deep and long and very passionate like in a movie. I had never kissed anybody quite like that nor felt anything quite like that before.

"I think I could love you forever," I said.

"You blow my mind!" he said.

We kissed again, although I felt uncomfortable. We were so obvious, in
public, sitting up in a tree making out in broad daylight.

"Let's go," Steve said suddenly.

"Why? What's wrong?"

"I want to make love to you."

He crawled down out of the tree and then helped me jump down. We
hugged but I couldn't breathe or speak.

Silently we drove back to Piedmont. No one was home so we went
through the vertical window and straight to the bedroom with the
two twin beds. Steve got undressed except for his underwear and
sat on the bed watching as I slowly got naked in front of him. I'd
been naked before with my last boyfriend, except for our underwear.
A couple times in fact.

I lay down on the bed with Steve and we began making out hot and
heavy and then he was on top of me pulling off his underwear,
spreading my legs, and trying to push himself inside me. I felt my
eyes roll to the back of my head.

He kept trying but it would not go in.

"I'm sorry," he said.

"It's okay."

"Am I hurting you?"

"A little."

"I'm sorry."

I wriggled out from under him. "It's not your fault. I can't relax."

I got up and started dressing. "Deanna and Ari might come back any
minute."

"So? They wouldn't care if we're in here."

"I can't," I said.

"You aren't still a virgin, are you?" he asked in disbelief.

"Yes," I sighed.

"I am so sorry. I wish I had known. I had no idea. I just figured you being
a friend of Deanna's that you'd been around. You know, been with
several guys already."

I felt like throwing up and crying all at the same time but I fought the urge to do either one.

Steve put his pants on and sat on the bed. "Come and sit here beside me."

I did as he asked. He put his arm around me.

"I feel like a freak."

He laughed. "Let's just pretend this never happened. Okay?"

"Okay."

"Your first time should be special and I want to make it up to you. Come back to San Francisco with me and stay the night. I'll take you to the airport tomorrow."

"What about Deanna? I've hardly seen her?"

"She won't mind. She's been wanting us to meet. She's probably happy we hit it off."

I flung my arms around Steve and kissed him hard.

Thank God, I get a second chance.

"Good," he said. "That settles it. Get your things and you can leave her a note."

What had been romantic and sensual so far was no comparison to riding with Steve in his VW back across the Bay Bridge and into the magical city of San Francisco.

Up and down the hills we went and he stopped at the top of each hill so I could take in the breathtaking views of the bay in every direction. Three- and four-story Victorians in unbroken bands followed the slopes and valleys, all lit up and twinkling as the sun started setting over the bay.

We stopped at Fisherman's Wharf and Steve bought fresh salmon for supper.

And then we went to his place on Roosevelt Avenue just over the hill from the Haight where just the day before Deanna and I had romped around high on acid.

His tiny apartment was actually the lower floor of a big house, and partly built into the side of the hill. Seventy-five steps lead up to his front door from the street where we parked. Twenty-five more steps continue on around the side of his place and further up the hill to the entrance of the main house where the road manager for Country Joe and the Fish lived.

Needless to say, Steve had one hell of a view from the big picture window in

his living room. There was a low bench with a cushion on it under the
window and next to that is his stereo and albums. The kitchen and
dining area were tiny. Barely large enough for two. Three stairs lead
up to his bed and the bathroom. Everything was painted glossy black.
"I see a red door and I want to paint it black," the Rolling Stones' lyrics
played in my head. I can't believe I'm with this man in his apartment,
was all I could think.
"Let's have a glass of wine," Steve said.
"Alright. I'll try anything once."
"You don't drink wine?"
"No, not really. I've had beer. And I got drunk on rum and coke once really
bad. I'm only eighteen, you know."
"That didn't stop me when I was eighteen," Steve said.
"I prefer grass or hash. Or acid. Cannibinal. Mostly grass."
"That's great. I told Deanna I won't date any girl who's straight. Here you
go," Steve said, and handed me a glass of white wine.
"Thanks." I took a sip. "Tastes good."
"It's a gewürztraminer."
"A what?"
"A German wine."
"How do you spell that?"
Steve showed me the bottle.
"Wow. Far out. I think you're place is really neat."
Steve came closer and kissed me. I kissed him back.
"I'll put on some music. Do you like jazz?"
"I don't know. My Aunt Frankie has some Eartha Kitt records and also
Nancy Wilson that I like."
"Ever heard of Miles Davis or John Coltrane or Ben Webster?"
I shook my head.
"I think you'll like this. It's Stanley Turrentine playing 'Willow Weep for Me.'"
I did like it. The music soothed me and aroused me at the same time. I
sipped more wine.
"Take your boots off and relax," Steve said.

I did as he said.

He filled my glass with more wine.

We sat and listened to the music and drank wine as the sun went down and
then he started kissing the back of my neck, my ears, and my throat.

"Let's go upstairs," he said.

I swallowed the last bit of wine in my glass and silently followed him.

Steve undressed and then slowly undressed me which really turned me on.
It's not like I didn't want sex. I wanted it with every guy I liked. Neal, Jim,
Jack, Craig, Greg, Paul, Grant, Rick, and the two Toms. I wanted it more
with some than others. And a couple of them, if not all of them, definitely
wanted to have sex with me. But something always stopped me. Not out
of virtue, either. Out of fear. Sheer, unadulterated terror. And I was too
embarrassed to tell anybody about it.

I laid back on the bed and Steve started kissing my toes, then my knees
and thighs, and then he skipped over my crotch to my stomach. I kept
my eyes closed and began squirming with anticipation and also anxiety
about the inevitable act.

He slowly pushed my legs apart with his.

I tried to relax.

He started humping me and kissing me all over and going faster and faster
and next thing I know he shoved himself inside me. I stuffed the pillow in
my mouth to keep from screaming.

And then he just went kind of crazy, humping away, up and down, and
breathing really hard.

Will he ever stop? This is getting boring. I don't feel a thing now. At least I'm
not a virgin anymore. What was I so afraid of? God, when will he ever
stop? I'm starting to feel claustrophobic.

And then it was all over. He had satisfied himself and flopped over on his
back beside me on the bed.

"That was great," he said.

"Yeah," I mumbled.

"Now it's your turn to come."

"That's okay," I said. "I'm fine. Really."

"You sure?"

"Positive. Yeah. I'm fine."

"Was everything else okay?"

"Yeah, fine. Great."

Steve got up out of the bed. "You were a virgin alright. There's blood on the sheet."

"Oh no, I'm sorry!"

"It's all right. It's been a long time since I made love to a virgin. I'm going to start dinner. You just stay there and relax."

Steve slid into his jeans and went downstairs.

And I started to shake.

And shake.

Scared? Overwrought? Tired? I can't feel anything. All I know is my body is shaking uncontrollably.

"Want some more wine?" Steve called from the kitchen three steps away.

"Not right now. Thanks."

Maybe if I just breathe deep and slow.

The shaking continued. I couldn't slow it down much less stop it.

Now I'm getting scared. I wish I could call my mother but she thinks I'm with Deanna. And what would I say anyway? She's always pounded into me that sex is beautiful only when you're married. Guess she was right. Now I've ruined my reputation. Now I'm no good.

"Steve! Could you come here for a minute?"

It took him five seconds.

"Are you sick or something?"

"I don't know. I'm shaking and I can't stop." I threw the sheet off me. "Look. I can't stop. I'm scared."

"Wow. I don't know what to do." Steve sat down beside me and put his arm around me but I kept on shaking. "Maybe I better call a doctor."

"No, don't do that. It's got to pass in a little while."

"Just stay in bed and try to relax."

He went back to the kitchen and continued making dinner.

I kept on shaking. Even my teeth were banging together.

"Dinner's ready."

"I can't eat."

"God, Steed. This has been going on for an hour."

"You go ahead and eat. I'll be fine. Really. It's got to stop sometime."

Steve put on some classical music that sounded soft and gentle.

"I'm right down here at the table if you need me."

The shaking continued. I fell asleep or passed out. I came to when I heard
Steve talking on the telephone.

"I don't know what's wrong," he said. "All I know is we had intercourse and
then she started shaking. And it's been going on for hours."

There was a pause as the person on the other end of the line spoke.

"Yes."

Pause.

"No."

Pause.

"I'll bring her right in. Thank you."

"What's going on?" I cried.

"That was a nurse at the hospital. She said to bring you to the emergency room."

It stopped.

The shaking stopped as soon as he said I had to go to the hospital.

"It's over. I'm not shaking anymore."

"Really?" Steve appeared beside the bed. "Jesus, you had me scared. You've
been shaking forever. I didn't know what I was going to do. Christ, it's
three in the morning."

"Sorry."

"You hungry?"

"Not really. I'm pretty wasted. If it's okay with you I'd like to try and get some
sleep."

"Okay. I'll take the couch and that way I won't bother you."

"Thanks. My plane leaves at ten in the morning."

"I'll set the alarm."

"Goodnight, Steve. Sorry I ruined dinner."

"Forget it. I'm just glad you're okay."

He sounded both relieved and disappointed.

22

I stared at the rain falling heavily on the apple orchard outside.

Gravenstein apples, to be exact. Practically the only place in the world where they grow. At least something thrives here, I thought to myself.

"So tell me more," Chris, my therapist, said.

"Whoever said 'All is change' was full of shit," I lamented. "Nothing ever changes."

"How so?" Chris asked.

"I'm here, aren't I? In therapy again after twelve years."

"So what does bring you here today?"

"I've got writer's block," I declared. "Haven't written in I don't know when."

"Writer's block? Have you always suffered from it?" I haven't heard that euphemism before. Is that why you went to therapy twelve years ago?"

That stopped me cold. At first I thought she was being sarcastic. I burst into tears. But Chris sat quietly with a kind look on her face, waiting patiently. I took a deep breath.

"We don't have sex," I blurted out.

"I see."

"It's my fault," I continued. "Steve wants it but I don't."

"There's two of you involved."

"That's what the therapist said twelve years ago. I suppose that means he has to be here too," I sighed.

"Not at all," Chris replied. "Only you can help you. And I am here for you. Your husband will have to help himself."

"That's a relief."

"So tell me, why don't you want sex?"

"The thing is," I slowly confessed, "I do want it. Sometimes I feel like I'm going to burn up with desire."

"But not for Steve," Chris stated.

"How did you know?" I flushed with embarrassment. "I want anybody but him."

"Have you had an affair?"

"No! Of course not," I cried.

"Maybe you should."

"I can't do that," I said, shocked that she would suggest such a thing.

"Why not?"

"I'm married."

"Are you? Are you really married? It doesn't sound like it. You might have a marriage license but that isn't what makes a marriage."

I stared at her. I didn't know what to say. Finally she spoke. "Problems with intimacy usually indicate a damaged childhood."

"What?" I exclaimed. "My childhood was perfectly normal."

I thought to myself, We were a perfectly normal family. I had a mother and a father…well, that was until they divorced… and my older brother, Will. We lived in a middle class neighborhood in Southern California and I went to good public schools with accelerated classes for smart kids like myself. My father worked and my mother stayed home and we always had three square meals a day. Sometimes we even went out to eat or to the drive-in movies. I got new clothes every year at the beginning of school…until the divorce.

I walked to and from school through clean, safe streets. Well, there was that one time when I was four or five when I walked to the Alpha Beta market with a neighbor girl and forgot to tell my mother. She beat me on my bare legs all the way home with a yardstick until it broke.

My friend, Marianne, and I roller-skated up and down the sidewalk in front of the tract of houses where we all lived. I joined the Brownies and later the Girl Scouts, and earned lots of money babysitting for the neighbors' children. But then, there was the time in 4th Grade when I started a Hate Club against Sharon Uster. We used to be friends. Her family was Catholic and I loved going to her house and seeing the statues of Jesus and Mary on her dresser, and the cross above the bed she slept in with her big sister. One day when nobody was home she and I played boy and girl on the bed. I guess we were about nine years old. We didn't get naked or anything but we practiced kissing. I'd be on top and she'd be the girl. Then we switched places and she'd be the boy kissing me with her big teeth pushing into my lips. In class, she always got straight A's and was the teacher's pet, which made me feel bad. It was almost the end of the school year and I couldn't stand it anymore. So I formed the club but only one girl joined. Of course, my teacher told my mother who immediately came to the school and made me stand in front of the class and apologize to Sharon. It was so hard to do because I was crying and everybody looked at me like there was something really wrong with me I just didn't understand. My mother then dragged me home and grounded me for the whole summer. I couldn't leave the house or go anywhere or have any company or play with anybody or anything. Most days I went to the far front corner of our yard and sat on the curb out of view of the kitchen window. It was as far away from home I could get without getting into trouble.

My brother never let me forget he was bigger and stronger than me. When no one was home he would start tormenting me, and when I ran, he'd chase me through the house while I screamed holy terror. Then he'd corner me and get me on the floor and sit on top of me and tickle me while I fought and screamed and choked until I'd pee my pants. That seemed to make him happy; then he'd get off me and walk away, leaving me there on the floor crying. I can't remember, I don't remember much about those attacks, but I guess there were times during the encounters that the phone rang because for years after that, whenever I was home by myself and the phone rang I would get hysterical and start crying and never answer it. For years I was terrified of the dark. I couldn't explain why. I had to have a nightlight in my room. And there were months when my mother had to get in bed with me so I could go to sleep. Is that a normal childhood?

One time, Will held me down in the backyard and I screamed for help, but the dog started licking the inside of my mouth and Will laughed and laughed while I gagged and choked and cried. One day, years later, after the divorce, when we were older and Mom was still at work, Will took the big butcher knife and threatened to cut off my arm. I don't remember what triggered his anger. I was mad at him, but I felt so hopeless that I told him to go ahead and cut it off and then I would run away. And then Mom would come after him. That stopped him cold. We never spoke of it after that. I never told Mom. And he never tried anything like that again. He just grew more and more aloof and barely acknowledged me or Mom after awhile.

My father had a good job with Kraft Foods as a salesman. He only went through the 8th Grade so he did well for himself. We ate a lot of that boxed macaroni-and-cheese. I liked my mother's homemade kind better. My father wore suits and ties and everything went towards making sure he was well dressed. Mom sent his white dress shirts out to be starched and ironed by a woman named Germaine who did that for a living. Neither Mom nor I could iron them to meet his satisfaction.

I bought ties and tie tacks every year for his birthday, Father's Day, and Christmas. He would stand in the living room beside the sliding glass door that went out onto the back patio and clip his fingernails so they were just so. He polished his leather dress shoes every night. And every morning my mother made him his breakfast of two fried eggs, bacon or sausage, toast with butter and jelly, and coffee. No one ever talked. He never asked one thing about me or school or anything else. I would sit there in my pajamas watching as he bit into his toast and the dark purple stuff would ooze between the small gap between his two front teeth. Then off he'd go in the car, his suit jacket swinging on a hanger on the hook in the back seat as he sped around the corner and disappeared. I always wondered where he went.

In the evenings I stood at the front door window watching for him to
come back around that corner. He always drove with one hand on
the wheel---casual, relaxed, confident, and looking very satisfied.
Meantime, my mother grew more uptight, impatient, and volatile
with us kids. She took care of the house, the grocery shopping, all
the cooking, washing and ironing, and cleaning. We had chores
and I helped with most all of that. Plus she had to take Will to the
doctor for his asthma which once turned to pneumonia and he had
to be in the hospital, and then he had Osgood-Schlatter disease
and there was a lot of doctor visits with that, plus driving me to the
orthodontist for four years for braces.

My father got a bigger and better job with Folger's Coffee and had all
of L.A. as his territory. He and my mother started drinking Folger's
Coffee from then on. And I kept buying him ties, tie tacks, and now
cufflinks for his good white shirts that were better than the cheaper
ones with buttons on the cuffs like he used to wear. By then I had
developed breasts, and for some reason I couldn't understand, he
started criticizing everything about me. My hair, my posture, my way
of talking and laughing. He never touched me. My mother joined in
with him, "Looks like a cat's been sucking on your hair, Steed." And
then the perfect family bubble popped.

He shacked up with a younger woman and moved out and I never felt
more horrible in my life. I felt totally responsible somehow. Plus all
the shame he brought onto the family and all the neighbors talking. I
remember feeling so confused and betrayed. Later his girlfriend got
pregnant so he totally abandoned us, divorced my mother, and married
her. He took all the money with him too, plunging us into poverty.

My brother had a job and his own car by then. He stayed with his friends
a lot, leaving me and Mom to our own devices. So both males in my
family pretty much disappeared. Still, I always tried to patch things
up somehow. On occasion our father called from the other town
where he lived with his new and improved family to talk to me. I
remember telling him to forget about me. I was alright. To please

make an effort to talk to Will who needed him. He seemed surprised and said he would. But he never did.

My mother had to get work. Although she had a high school diploma she hadn't worked at a steady job for at least fifteen years. And in those days employers didn't look kindly upon women without husbands. No one looked kindly upon a divorcee. Mom had to leave the house at five in the morning to drive the two hours to the job so she could solder parts for jet bombers on an assembly line at Douglas Aircraft. No more new clothes for school. No more new anything. In the blink of an eye, the world branded me as "a child from a broken home." I pretty much stopped eating, developed anemia, and a "spastic bowel" as the doctor called it. I never once, not ever, saw my parents be affectionate with each other nor were they ever that way with me or Will. The only touch was from my mother who raged a good deal of the time during those early years, which meant a backhand across the face, or the belt, or a spanking. I learned to shut down, keep quiet, keep a low profile, do as I was told, and retreat to my room where I would write poetry. By the time I was fifteen, I firmly declared I would never cry again. When I was sixteen, I started smoking grass. And later, I dropped acid, smoked hashish, and took cannibinal. Instead of new clothes for school, I now wore the same dress five days in a row and refused to wear a bra. I wrote dozens and dozens of poems. And vowed to never have children.

"Steed, take this," Chris said.

She handed me a long-handled mirror.

"Cover your nose and mouth lightly with your hand. Now look in the mirror."

I did as she said and stared at my reflection.

"Look at your eyes. What do you see?"

Terror. Pain. Shock. The eyes of a soft but wounded animal. Trapped, injured, and petrified.

I couldn't speak.

"You see what I mean now? About a damaged childhood?" Chris softly asked.

I nodded as I started to cry.

She handed me the box of Kleenex.

"So it is my fault that Steve and I don't have sex," I said.

"No, it isn't."

"I guess I'm frigid."

Chris laughed. "No woman is frigid. It's the man who makes her so. But if it's the right man, he will make sure she feels loved and appreciated. And sexually satisfied and fulfilled."

Her words gave me hope.

"Really?" I exclaimed. "So maybe all this time Steve has been the wrong man?"

"I don't know that," Chris answered. "But I can tell you one thing. Any man who keeps blaming his partner for what goes on in the bedroom has issues of his own that he either refuses to deal with or is in complete denial about."

"I don't see how that could be. He always wants sex."

"That's convenient for him, isn't it?" Chris replied. "He wants what he wants when he wants it. There's no regard for you anywhere in there that I can see. But it doesn't really matter now. You are on your own path of self-discovery and healing and embracing the person and woman you truly are. Everything else will change accordingly."

I must have looked at her with a worried expression.

"Don't worry, Steed. It will all work out for the best."

When I got home, Steve was engrossed making dinner. This time he didn't ask how the therapy session went.

Neither of us spoke as I stood there in the kitchen watching him.

Finally I blurted out, "I had a damaged childhood."

"What does that mean?" he asked, not making eye contact.

I think he was holding his breath too.

"I don't know," I slowly answered. "Abuse, I guess. Physical…emotional…"

I paused. It was so hard to say it.

"And probably sexual. Except I can't remember. I've buried it."

Steve stopped what he was doing and looked at me, nodding his head as if to say I told you so.

"Well, you know what's wrong with you now, so you can fix it," he said.

I suddenly felt a deep chill run through my body. It was now officially
my problem.

"Anything else?" he challenged. Meaning, did the therapist say anything
about him.

I shook my head. I didn't feel like talking any more. And if I did tell him what
she had said, he would just get angry and argue.

"Let me tell you what kind of day I had," he said, changing the subject.

I saw the movie, *Looking for Mr. Goodbar*, but that didn't stop me from going
to bars and clubs and picking up guys. It was a rite of passage I had to
carry out. I should have done it twenty years ago but I got married too
young, too soon.

It all began when Steve was out of town for a week. I got up the nerve to ask
Ken at work if he wanted to get together. He is a tall, good looking white
guy that works upstairs as a production assistant, mostly at night. I run the
TV station's traffic department downstairs during regular business hours.
I think I had seen him maybe twice and figured he was safe since I didn't
really know him. Anyway, he was game.

I took off work a little early and Ken came to my house late that afternoon
before he had to go to work. We barely talked. He knew what I wanted.

We rolled around on the living room floor like a couple of blind wrestlers so I
suggested we go to my bed. He knew I was married and I got the feeling
I wasn't the first married woman he had accommodated.

So there I was with my first lover—the first man I would have intercourse
with other than Steve—in broad daylight in the bed Steve and I sleep in.
There was no foreplay. No kissing. No talking. He shoved himself inside
me and humped away for a few minutes until he exploded. And then he
rolled off me and onto his back. The odor of his ejaculation strangled me.

I jumped up and ran to the bathroom to wash myself. When I came back Ken
was already dressed and headed toward the door. I followed him down
the hall, feeling sick to my stomach. It sure as hell wasn't what I thought
it would be like, nor did I feel any better.

Before he went out the door he turned to me and said, "You seem lonely. Don't you have any friends, like a girlfriend you could talk to?"

I blinked with astonishment. I didn't know what to say.

"I think you need a friend," he said matter-of-factly and left.

I became furious and rushed back to the bedroom and stripped the bed. His odor hung unpleasantly in the air. I opened the bedroom windows, put the sheets in the washing machine, and took a very hot and soapy shower, scrubbing myself over and over. I ran the sheets through a second cycle and burned incense in the bedroom. And then I made myself a strong gin and tonic.

Steve returned the next day. I sat on the bed while he unpacked, watching him closely to see if he smelled or suspected anything. He was oblivious as he talked about his trip and the meeting he had. That disturbed me even more as the events of the previous afternoon spun wildly around in my head.

I can't go on like this. It just isn't right. I don't want to hurt Steve. And I don't want to lie to him. I never have before and I'm not about to start now. But I can't tell him about my experience either. I feel so alone.

Several days later, I confessed all to my therapist whom I now saw once a week and had been for two years.

"Sounds like your lover gave you something valuable after all," Chris said.

"What do you mean?" I said, aghast. He gave me his smelly semen is what he gave me, I thought to myself.

"He saw you. That is more than Steve has done. He saw who you are and acknowledged it."

I could feel the tears coming on strong.

Chris smiled benevolently and handed me the all-too familiar box of Kleenex.

"Steed, he said you are lonely. Is he right?"

I nodded through my tears.

She nodded with me. "He said you need a friend. Is he right?"

I shrugged. Steve has always been my one and only friend. How could I betray him?

I dried my eyes and blew my nose.

"I feel terrible," I said.

"Why? Because you want something more than what you have now?"

"Yes. It's always been just me and Steve."

"You and him against the world?"

"Something like that."

"But you're not happy?"

I shook my head. "No, I'm not. And I feel terrible because I think I should be happy with Steve."

"Steed, listen to yourself," Chris said firmly.

"What?"

"You think you should be happy," Chris stated.

"Yes. With Steve," I insisted.

"You think you should be happy," Chris repeated.

"Yes, with…"

Chris interrupted me.

"You think you should be happy," she slowly repeated. "Just hear that for now, okay? You think you deserve to be happy. To be happier than you are now. Just take that in for a few minutes. I'll be right back."

Chris left the room and I took a couple deep breaths.

My whole life pretty much has been with Steve. We've been together almost sixteen years. And now I've cheated on him, just like my father cheated on my mother. I'm no good, just like him. But I'm not getting divorced like they did. I will not be a divorced woman. I've never been with anyone else but Steve. And that's just it. I feel something's missing. I don't know what it is. But I do know I want to be with other men. That sounds awful. But I need to be with other men. I don't understand it exactly but I do know I have to do this. It's the only way I can get to myself somehow. And the only way I can do that, and live with myself, is to move out.

Chris returned. "So what do you think," she asked.

I sighed.

"Ready to take the next step?"

"I guess," I replied.

"This is a process, Steed. You're on a journey that most people don't take. They're too afraid. It takes tremendous courage to do what you are doing."

I laughed nervously.

"So, your homework is to go out with a friend one evening. You mentioned a couple gals at work you like. See if one of them wants to go have a drink after work. Or go to a movie Friday night. Okay?"

"Okay," I agreed reluctantly.

"And I want a full report when I see you next week."

"Alright."

I started out the door.

"Steed!" Chris called. "Have fun!"

23

Friday morning it finally quit raining.

I finished my coffee and gathered up courage as I poured more coffee for Steve.

"I think today after work I'm going to go out with Charley," I mumbled.

"What?" Steve looked shocked.

"Charley. She's the woman I told you about who does all the graphic design for the station."

"Since when are you two such good friends?" Steve demanded.

I felt myself getting hot around the face so I started clearing the table.

"I've known her quite awhile," I said defensively. "She's not married and doesn't have a boyfriend right now so I thought it would be nice if she had somebody to go out with." I was shocked how easily the lie slipped from my lips. I promised myself I would not go down that road.

"Then let's all go out together," Steve said.

I took a deep breath. "No," I heard myself say.

Steve looked surprised. "Why not?"

"I think I just want a girls' night out. Besides, you and I don't have to do everything together, do we?" I tried to remain calm.

Steve stood up and shoved the chair into the table. "I don't get it," he said angrily.

I couldn't breathe. He had me cornered in the kitchen and I was afraid he would hit me.

"I don't understand why all of a sudden you want to go out without me, Steed."

"I'm not choosing her over you," I said, stumbling over my words. "I just
    need to do different things."
"Like what other things?" he demanded.
I snapped. "I'm just going out with a friend!" I cried. "I need some space, okay?"
"What the hell are you talking about?" Steve screamed. "You've got your
    space! You have your own room to write in! You have your job you
    go to everyday! You're free to do whatever you want! What kind of
    goddam space do you want anyway?"
"I'm suffocating! We're not Siamese twins, you know! We're not joined at
    the hip! We don't have to do everything together all the time!"
"You need space. You need to go out," Steve sneered. "What about what
    I need? Do I ever get what I need? Hell no, I don't. I've been waiting
    for years for you to come around and now you tell me you want to go
    out with your girlfriends. Well then, go! Go out with whoever the hell
    you want to! I don't give a shit!"
Steve stomped down the hall to his office and slammed the door.
I finished getting ready for work and left quietly, shaking all over.

———————

Charley and I sat in the restaurant connected to the cinema quad
    downtown. We had a table at one of the floor-to-ceiling windows.
    I enjoyed just sitting there watching all the people milling around
    the theater.
"I'm glad you were free to do something tonight," I said. I poured us more wine.
"Yeah, this is cool," Charley replied. "I don't really have a girlfriend to pal
    around with. Seems like everyone's married but me."
"Oh my God!" I cried. "Speaking of married, there's my husband."
"Where?"
"The guy in the black leather jacket."
"Wow, he's really handsome."
"What is he doing here?" I asked out loud.
"Maybe he wants to see a movie," she said innocently.
"No, no. You don't understand. I went out without him, so now he's going

out, too, just to show me. Why did he have to come here?"

"I don't think he sees you, if that's what you're worried about."

"I hope not. It spoils everything."

"Do you want to leave?" Charley asked.

"Yes. Do you mind?"

"Of course not. Let's go over to Railroad Square. There's a neat club there. He'll never find you there."

"Great," I sighed.

"We can have some drinks and dance our asses off," she added as we slipped out the door.

Charley entered the club like the regular she was. Her wild, frizzy red hair, short tight skirt, long legs, and high heels preceded me and my short brown hair with highlights, turtleneck and jacket, jeans, and boots.

The place was dark and crowded and the music was loud. A live band was lit up in one corner of the room and lots of people were dancing.

We ordered margaritas, took a couple sips, and hit the dance floor. Charley and I just danced freestyle. We didn't need partners. We didn't need men. I hadn't felt this free in a long time.

"This reminds me so much of the Sixties when I was in high school!" I yelled over the music. "I used to go to places like the Shrine in L.A. and freak out under the strobe lights!"

"Me too!" she yelled back.

"Really? That is so far out! We were probably dancing next to each other!" Charley nodded and laughed.

"I saw people like John Mayall and The Doors and B.B. King! What a far out time that was!"

The band ended their set and took a break.

We went back to our drinks at the bar.

I looked across the room and locked eyes with one particular guy who had been watching me intensely. He smiled. I smiled and felt something stir inside me.

24

Steve never mentioned my night out with Charley and I never mentioned
I saw him at the movie theater.

I couldn't get Jackson Smith out of my mind—a long and lanky black
man about ten years younger than me with a wonderful smile.

When we met at the club, I told him my name was Denise. I don't know
why. It just popped out.

Jackson noticed the ring on my left hand and tapped it a couple times
with his finger.

"Yes, I'm married," I said. "Do you have a problem with that?"

"No," he replied. "I've got a girlfriend. Do you have a problem with that?"

I shook my head no. He gave me his phone number and told me where
he lived.

Two weeks later I got up my nerve to call him and we agreed to meet at
noon in the food court at the mall.

"I am going to explode if I don't go to bed with you," I declared.

He laughed. "Just say when."

"Now."

He stared at me.

"I'm serious. I don't have to be back to work for awhile."

"Where do you work?" he asked.

"It doesn't matter," I said, avoiding the question. "They can get along without me for a couple hours."

"Let's go to my place. You can follow me in your car."

"What about your girlfriend?"

"She happens to be out of town for a week, visiting her sister."

I pulled my car up behind his in front of an old wood-frame fourplex not far from the club where we had met.

Jackson draped his long arm around my neck and let it fall heavily against my breasts. He guided me up the wooden stairs to his one-room apartment. A large bed took up most of the room.

We started kissing immediately and undressing each other and then kissing and when we were both naked and lying down, he put on a condom. I looked at him. Does he think I'm dirty or something?

He noticed my expression. "I don't want to infect you with anything," he explained.

I hadn't even thought about that. I didn't really know about such things. As I admired his beautiful firm, dark body I really didn't care.

Tenderly, slowly, deeply, and passionately we lost ourselves in each other until it was almost two o'clock and I had to get back to work.

Jackson watched as I hurriedly dressed and said, "You have big thighs."

"Thanks a lot," I snapped back, feeling suddenly unappreciated and rejected.

"Calm down, Denise. I'm not saying I don't like them. They're just bigger than other women I've been with."

"Go to hell. Go be with them then."

"Come back here."

"No, I've got to go. I'm really late."

I rushed back into the office. One of the salesmen eyed me and said, "What happened to you?"

"I've been on a roller coaster," I quipped.

"Looks like you've been rode hard and put away wet."

"Very funny," I said as he sauntered off.

God, is it that obvious? I thought to myself. Pull yourself together. Steve will know something's up. What am I going to do? At least Jackson doesn't know my real name or where I work or live.

I woke up with a start at six a.m. The alarm was set for seven. Steve was
    sound asleep. I slowly slipped out of bed and went into the other
    room and dressed for jogging.
I tiptoed out of the house and took off running across the west end of
    town to Jackson's place. Without thinking, I ran up the stairs and
    knocked on his door. He eventually answered and was shocked to
    see me.
"Denise!"
"Can I come in? Please?"
He opened the door wider and let me in. All he had on were his scivvies.
    I threw my arms around him and we fell down on the bed. He pulled
    my shoes off and then my clothes. An hour later I jogged back
    home. It was seven-thirty. Steve was in the shower.
"Is that you, Steed?"
"Yeah! I went for a run!"
"I've got a meeting at eight-thirty."
"I'll make you some breakfast," I said.
I stood at the kitchen sink, feeling happy and alive and sick to my
    stomach all at the same time.
The phone rang then which was unusual for so early in the morning.
"Hello," I answered.
"Denise, I can see you."
"What?" I nearly screamed.
"I followed you. So now I know where you live. And I can see you there in
    the kitchen."
I panicked. I wasn't afraid of Jackson. I was afraid of what Steve would
    do if he found out.
"Listen, Jackson. It's over. I just now confessed to my husband about us," I
    lied. "I had to. He confronted me and I had to tell him or he was going
    to hit me. He said he'll kill whoever it is I'm screwing around with. I
    never told him your name. I promise I never will. But for your sake,
    stay away from me."
"Steed!" Steve called from the bathroom. "Was that the phone?"

"Yes! It's a problem at work! I don't know why they can't wait till I get there!"
I lied again.

"Denise, are you alright?"

"Jackson, listen to me," I whispered. "Don't ever call me or try to see me again. I'm begging you. For your own good. And mine too. He'll kill us both."

"Okay. Don't worry, I won't bother you again. Good luck," he said and hung up.

It's no use. I can't go on like this, I told myself. The deceit is killing me. I hate dishonesty. I hate having to lie. The only solution is to separate from Steve and do what I want to do out in the open. No more cheating or sneaking around or pretending. Maybe it's just something I need to get out of my system. Maybe if I just have my own place and some time to myself I can figure this all out. And then maybe the marriage will be better and I'll feel differently about Steve.

So I got rid of Jackson. I hated to see him go. He was my first black lover. His skin was beautiful. And so was the rest of him. And he was incredibly attentive. But he wouldn't be my last. Not by any means. Each one brought a tenderness I hadn't known. And excitement and adventure. Yet I was comfortable with them at the same time. Perhaps because I was on the outside looking in, much as they were. Not fitting in somehow. Always feeling alien, confused, curious, and longing to connect.

25

The days are getting shorter. It was already dark by the time I drove
home from my weekly therapy session with Chris.

The blinds in the house were still open and I could see Steve in the brightly
lit kitchen fixing supper. I felt sick to my stomach as I went inside.

"I'm home!" I called out and headed straight to the bathroom.

"I'll pour you some wine," Steve answered.

I stared at myself in the mirror. It's now or never, Steed. You will never
forgive yourself if you don't do this. And there isn't going to be any
better time than right now.

"So how was your day?" Steve asked as I entered the kitchen.

"Good," I said as I grabbed the glass of wine waiting for me on the counter.

"How was therapy?"

I took a long drink of wine. "Pretty heavy. But good."

"Hungry?"

"I guess."

"Good, because it's ready. So let's eat."

We sat down at the table. Actually I was starving. Steve poured us both
more wine.

"Do you think the therapy is helping you at all?" he asked.

"Definitely."

"Hmm, that's interesting. Because it doesn't seem to be helping things as far as you and I are concerned."

"And that's my fault, right?" I snapped.

"Hey, jump back! You're the one with the incest problems. Not me."

"Oh, right. Thanks for never letting me forget that either."

"I'm just saying I don't see things changing much between us."

"Well, they're about to," I said, swallowing hard.

He stared at me, waiting.

"Steve," I began as I trembled all over, "knowing what I know now about my damaged childhood and the likelihood of incest and everything, it just seems to me I'm not much good to you and haven't been, really. I've pretty much been a failure as a wife. I have amnesia about it all and may never remember, so I don't know if I ever can be whatever it is you want me to be."

"I want sex, like any other normal person. What the hell do you think?" Steve said.

"Like I said, I don't know if I can ever give you that," I said, talking even faster. "So I'm going to move out and get my own place. It'll just be for awhile. I'll rent something here in town and try to figure out my life and find out more who I am. You know, try to work on healing all this shit, and maybe be with other men."

"What?" he screamed.

I thought for sure he was going to hit me or throw his plate at my face like he's done before. One time he almost put my eye out. I just sat there and waited for it because I knew it wouldn't change what I had decided.

But he didn't make a move.

"You heard me," I continued. "I want to be with other men. And I don't want to sneak behind your back or lie or cheat. So I'm moving out. You can be with other women if you want. I don't care."

"This is fucking bullshit!" he exclaimed.

"I need to do this. I can't explain it but it's what I've got to do to for myself so I can heal."

In the fifteen years we had been married, I had never seen him so angry as at that moment.

"I didn't expect you to understand, Steve. But I didn't want to hurt you either. I wanted to be up front with you about this."

Without a word, Steve got up and methodically cleared the table and put
　　everything away while I sat there fighting back the tears.
Finally, he broke the silence. "So when is all this going to happen?"
"As soon as I can find a place."
"Good," he sneered. "The sooner the better."

The house was so quiet you would have thought I had it all to myself.
How weird to go through everything Steve and I own together and pick
　　out items to furnish my own place.
It felt strange.
It also felt exciting.
The first thing I moved was my desk—a door and two sawhorses. Also,
　　the bolt-on drafting lamp, my desk chair, all my writing books, my
　　electric typewriter and my old manual one I haul everywhere and
　　never use, assorted books including a couple of cookbooks, and
　　my clothes.
Someone loaned me a double bed to sleep on. I took my own pillow off
　　of our bed, and one set of sheets and a blanket along with two bath
　　towels with matching washcloths out of the linen closet.
I also took the rocking chair that my parents bought when they were
　　first married, a floor lamp, a set of dishes my mother gave me when I
　　was still in high school, a radio, the little TV and stand, a couple pots
　　and pans, an iron skillet, one of the good cutting knives and one of
　　the cutting boards, six forks, six knives, and six spoons. And one
　　pair of scissors.
Andrea, a mutual friend of ours, helped me move, which at first I thought
　　was really nice of her. I figured as a woman ten years older than me
　　who was in her fourth marriage, she understood my situation and
　　only wanted to help.
She and I carried boxes and small items up and down the hall past the
　　bedroom where Steve laid paralyzed on the bed. Every time I went
　　by I glanced in and there he was, still and stiff as a corpse. I couldn't

help thinking, What an odd thing to do. Why doesn't he just leave for the day? Or go in his office and shut the door? Or go for a walk? Instead he just lays there, useless and dramatic as always.

It wasn't long before I realized Andrea was helping get me out of the picture so she could get it on with Steve.

I don't care. She can have him. I am ready to be in my own place, living alone, for the first time in my life. I'm thirty-four years old!

Andrea went on to my apartment with her pick-up loaded. I went into the kitchen to see if there was anything else I could use.

Steve wandered in like someone who just crawled out from under a rock.

I felt giddy and excited and sad and confused and terrified.

"If you need anything, just let me know," he said weakly.

"Can I take some of the food and a couple bottles of wine?"

"Sure."

I walked over to the refrigerator.

"You know, you can come here anytime you want. It's still your house, too."

"Thanks, Steve. I appreciate that," I said and opened the refrigerator door.

At that moment, something clicked. Something deep like an earthquake fault shifted inside me.

And all of a sudden out of nowhere, a massively heavy door opened on the tomb of my past. A barrage of buried memories bombarded me. Everything blurred as this other dimension literally swallowed me up.

I staggered to the counter to hold on as a violent wave of excruciating visions reverberated through me.

"What is it? "What's wrong?" Steve cried out, though to me he sounded miles away.

The utter and inescapable terror of being physically violated by my own father who I loved and trusted came blasting to the surface of my mind.

I heard myself howling in anguish—the deep, primeval moan of a wounded animal filled with pain and terror—as I relived the acute betrayal that had left me feeling so horribly abandoned and so utterly alone for thirty years.

I screamed, moaned, howled, and sobbed with despair and grief as the amnesia that had held me so long in its clutch finally lifted.

There was our backyard in Southern California that went a long ways back from the house to a dirt alley. There were lots of big bushes and trees back there.

My father was teaching me to ride my bicycle without the training wheels. He ran alongside me holding onto one of the handlebars and then he would let go. We did this a few times. And then after riding a short distance on my own, I crashed in the dirt. I had a dress on and scraped my bare knees so badly they were bleeding, which made me cry.

Before I knew what was happening, my father pulled me out from under the bicycle and into the thick bushes. I thought he was going to spank me for falling off the bike or for getting my dress all dirty, although he had never laid a hand on me before.

Instead he pulled down my panties and started fiddling with me with his fingers. I cried now because I was terrified. I remember all he said was, "Don't cry, don't cry, don't cry."

I didn't understand what was happening. He moved quickly, unzipping his pants with one hand while he held me down with the other. And then he started licking me down there while he had one hand inside his own pants. I kept crying and choking and it seemed to go on forever.

Apparently I passed out because the next thing I knew I was lying there in the bushes, my panties pulled back up, my scraped knees crusted with dried blood and dirt, and my cat was now curled up next to me. I knew my mother was going to be furious that I got so dirty and probably give me a spanking.

A feeling of extreme aloneness consumed me. I felt absolutely forsaken. I never wanted to crawl out from there. Not ever.

I remember making a vow that I would never trust anybody or anything ever again except animals.

Then memories of life in Oregon loomed into my consciousness.

I remembered my mother making me go into the bedroom in the morning to say goodnight to my father before I could go out and play. He worked the graveyard shift and slept during the day.

She would push me inside and close the door. And then she'd go back to the
kitchen, which was way on the other side of the big old house we lived in.

My father pulled me into the bed and fondled me and I pleaded with him to
let me go. I was scared every time.

He put his hand over my mouth and pretty much did the same things to me
he had done the year before we moved to Oregon. Over and over and
over and over I continued to be abandoned and betrayed.

That's when I learned to leave my body whenever any man touched it.

And now it was all out.

Exhumed.

Exorcised.

Every painful memory regained.

The unknown cause of decades of inner torment now excised and exposed
to the light.

The princess had finally found the pea.

The sickening, rotten, forbidden pea of truth.

It would take fifteen more years for the truth to illuminate — and eliminate —
the darkness.

For certain parts to heal and other parts to grow.

Fifteen years shedding the old skin entirely.

And growing into a new one.

EPILOGUE

Victoria, British Columbia — February, 2011

My hotel room faces Inner Harbour.

I chose Laurel Point Inn so I could sit and stare at the water.

I don't know why I expected a placid, quiet body of water to reflect
upon. It is, after all, a harbor where boats and ships and yachts and
hydroplanes go in and out all day.

So maybe I don't need placid.

I actually enjoy watching the water traffic come and go. It's like watching
thoughts with detachment come and go during meditation.

This is the first vacation I've had in I-don't-know-how-long, and the first one
I've taken since I've been on my own. And it's First Class all the way.

I had to escape the Texas drought. After living there for fifteen years,
you'd think a person would get used to it. But not when it hits ninety
degrees in January and there hasn't been a drop of rain for months.

Besides seeking relief from the dryness and heat, I couldn't think of a
better way to celebrate ending a six-year love affair than to take
myself far, far away to somewhere special.

I knew better and fought like hell to avoid Martin who was married. But
in the end I became a classic textbook case of older divorcee on the
rebound, free yet bewildered. Especially after thirty years of marriage.

Turns out it is very common for divorced women to get involved with married men. I had no idea until I divulged my situation to various women, including my mother.

For three years I tangled myself up with Martin and then spent the next three years trying to disentangle myself. But one extremely important thing I learned, I had no sexual problems. What a shock and a blessing. What freedom. Especially after all those years of blame, guilt, and despair in my marriage.

Prior to the affair, six years had passed without sex or affection of any kind between me and my husband, Steve. We had become mutually resigned to our life together being this way. Yet I never could accept it. Deep inside I just knew there had to be more.

A horrid, chronic sense of unease plagued me all the time as did self-recrimination, doubt, and depression. Bouts of loneliness came and went like the tide. One-night stands were no longer an option. I'd outgrown those from when I was separated from Steve fifteen years earlier. After the first few, they became boring and too much trouble. And generally unsatisfying.

I didn't consider having an affair either. I had no desire. I didn't even feel like a woman. And certainly not a wife. I felt more like a female zombie roommate. Steve and I had exhausted therapy years ago. I'd had three straight years of it and so had he. Plus we went one year as a couple. Now, any attempt to discuss anything turned into a raging argument. The relationship boiled down to love it or leave it. So I left.

Since I was 14, I have taken many paths in search of answers: LSD; yoga; studies of Native American and Eastern philosophies; living in a Zen monastery; years of Zen meditation and practice; psychotherapy; years of deep bodywork; reverence for Virgin Mary; devotion to Nature; going to college at thirty-six for writer's block and inadvertently earning a degree; consultations with professional psychics and astrologers; becoming a Siddha Yoga devotee; years of Resonance Repatterning; and practicing The Work on a daily basis. And always writing throughout. Trying, trying, trying to get to the truth. And now I'm finally there.

Before Martin preyed upon me, I met a rancher who broke the deadly
    spell. He didn't plan it and I didn't seek it. But it happened. Meeting
    him inexplicably awakened my long-latent sexuality. Physically,
    psychically, the lid blew off. I'd been buried alive for so long, and
    suddenly the heavy sarcophagus blasted open. The rancher wasn't
    anything special. He was just a nice man. And timing is everything.
Afterwards, electrical jolts ran through my body when I least expected
    it. At one point, I sat on the edge of my bed unable to walk, I was
    shaking so badly. And I had never done anything but talk to him.
Fortunately, he called me one night. He'd had a fight with his girlfriend
    and was home by himself on his 5,000-acre ranch. He'd also been
    drinking a little. I grabbed a bottle of wine and drove two hours
    through the vast countryside at midnight to get to him. And luckily,
    he wasn't too drunk to take me to bed and free me from my six-year
    dry spell. It was right out of a Country Western song.
After that, he made up with his girlfriend and I succumbed to Martin.
    I knew for sure I could never go back to Steve. There was no reason
    to prolong the marriage any longer. With great fear and dread and
    excitement, I filed for divorce.
And here I am, six years later, free of two relationships that had to end.
    I finally had the clarity and courage to terminate them both. And
    jump into the unknown — aloneness.
Rain, fog, mist, and saltwater all appeal to me right now. So fresh and
    cool and clean. As each year passes in Texas, I miss the ocean more
    and more. Interesting that I should end up in Texas after all the
    many places I've lived and traveled:
Anaheim, California; Myrtle Creek, Oregon; La Habra Heights,
    California; San Francisco; the redwoods of Northern California;
    a Zen monastery; Santa Monica; L.A.; an island in Maine; the
    Sonoran Desert in Tucson; the wine country of Northern California;
    Venice Beach.
And crisscrossing the country. Once by train from Seattle to Knoxville.
    And by car through Oregon and Washington to attend a Dai-

Sesshin at the Vancouver Zen Center. And through Vermont, New Hampshire, upstate New York, Montreal, and Quebec.

One year we left L.A. and traveled by VW bus through Las Vegas at four in the morning to stay cool because the bus had no A/C, on to Utah, Idaho, turned right at Wyoming, drove east through South Dakota, Minnesota (Blue Earth), Chicago, Indiana, across Ohio and Pennsylvania to New York and up the coast through Rhode Island and Massachusetts all the way to Maine.

After a year on the island in Maine, and the coldest winter there in fifty years, with no snow, we headed back down through Philadelphia, Baltimore, D.C., Virginia, North and South Carolina, across Georgia and Alabama through Mobile to Biloxi where the gulf laps literally at the town's feet. Then on through Baton Rouge and the bayous, Houston, across Texas on I-10, through New Mexico and Arizona to Tucson, where we stopped for a year. (I call that move Out of the Freezer and into the Oven.)

There were also numerous in-depth travels or lengthy stays — many of them by myself—in all sorts of places such as Paris, Fontainebleau, Athens, Rome, New York City, Boston, Zurich, the Swiss Alps, Florence, Venice (several times), London and southern England (interviewing American expatriates), Istanbul, the Greek island of Patmos, and three months in a VW bus throughout Mexico clear down to Yucatan and Chiapas and back up through El Paso, New Mexico, Colorado, and over the Rockies westward.

Always searching, traveling, looking, studying, experiencing, exploring — much of it sheer freedom since I had no children. But I did have an incurable restlessness which the therapist pointed out as, "Rest less; minus rest; unable to rest until something is resolved." Plus I had wanderlust since age twelve which I now think I inherited from my great-grandmother, Rhoda Steed Sistrunk.

Thanks to her, she broke the mold and fled life in Mississippi with her lover. They moved from east to west across Texas in her relentless pursuit for freedom but having babies every two years thwarted her dreams and made her mean. My grandmother was one of those nine babies, born in the middle of Texas, not far from where I now live. But the family kept on going until they couldn't go any further west which was California where eventually my mother was born, and then me.

When I went to Mississippi, I stood in the Doty Springs Cemetery next to Doty Springs Baptist Church (where, I discovered, my great-great-great grandfather had been a preacher for fifty years). I was stunned to find three consecutive generations of my family buried there, along with their stories—including Rhoda's many brothers and sisters which I never knew she had.

But Rhoda's not there. She's buried somewhere in California. So is her daughter Ann, my grandmother. And so is Ann's daughter Kitty, my mother. But none are near each other. No family grave for them.

End of story.

As for me, I went east.

Smack dab in the middle of Texas.

The truth finally setting me free.

Free, free, free at last.

Finally comfortable in my own skin.

My own sensual, sexual female skin.

Not always content, though.

Longing more and more for the ocean.

The sound and smell and surge of the sea.

And sometimes I'm lonely.

Disconnected.

No roots, no ties.

No children.

But I made that choice.

And it's been a real trip.

I look at the harbor as I pick up my pen and start to write:

"I am the last daughter."

COMING AROUND

I hear myself scolding the child
            who is not there –
I am being the mother I am not.
The woman in me surges,
                    then wanes.
I see myself adorned
            in stepmother wickedness.
I hear the cry of a child
            who is not there –
I have been the terrible mother
                I am not.
The person in me lunges forth,
                Then drifts to a lull.
I see myself as I see my mother
            and her mother –
As my mother sees herself
            and her mother –
A hexed circle.
                I hear myself crying
                as the mother in me
                soothes
                The child I am.

RENÉE WALKER | *August 30, 1977*

THE AUTHOR

Renée Walker was born in Los Angeles.

Her poetry, short stories, essays, and plays have won awards and been produced and published in various newspapers, magazines, and literary journals including *Chicago Tribune*; *Denver Post*; *The Arizona Daily Star*; *San Francisco Bay Guardian*; *Westways Magazine*; *Venice West Review*; *Quarry*; *Event*; *Spectrum*; *The Panhandler*, *Tex!*; Actors' Theatre, Santa Rosa; and included in *Contemporary Women Poets: An Anthology of California Poets*.

In 2002, Renée was a Featured Author at the prestigious annual Texas Book Festival in Austin for her first book, *Texas Rangeland*.

Hill Country & Other Poems was selected by Women Writing the West as the 2006 Finalist of the WILLA Literary Awards for Poetry.

Renée's third book, *Around the Square: That's Mason*, is a collection of her weekly ruminations on life in a small town that she writes for the *Mason County News*.

Renée lives in Mason, Texas.